parallel lines

PART 1

KW PUBLISHING

www.kennywriter.com

Parallel Lines: Part 1

Edited by Stephen Rudolph

Cover design by Kenny Wright

Cover image © NYUSHA2014/bigstockphoto.com

First digital edition electronically published by KW Publishing, July 2015

First print edition published by KW Publishing, July 2015

Printed by CreateSpace, Charleston SC

Foreword

This book is a true collaboration between Ben Boswell and me (Kenny Wright), although credit for the initial idea goes to Ben. He came up with the clever idea of two individuals embarking on mutual flings. Beyond that, we had no plan, just a blank screen and our wild imaginations.

You'll find an interview and more thoughts on my blog (www.kennywriter.com), which have been repeated at the end of the second book, so I'll keep this part brief.

Yes, it was a great experience. Yes, we both really did contribute equally. The exercise in passing a story like this back and forth challenged both of us to step up our game, try some new things, and write in situations that we don't always normally gravitate to.

And I actually challenge you, the reader, to even try and guess what he wrote versus what I wrote.

Special thanks to longtime readers Stephen and RP for their help catching typos.

If you enjoy Parallel Lines and want to see more from the two of us, let us know. Write a review or two. Send us an email (kennywright.writer@gmail.com and ben.boswell.author@gmail.com), or find us on social media (@kennywriter and @benboswellaut or www.benboswell.com) and say, "Hey, more please!"

But for now, kick back and enjoy. You're in for a ride.

One

It had to be an optical illusion. Something about the way the fabric of his trousers shifted or the way the pinstripes down around his pockets and thighs merged. Something. Because it had to be an optical illusion. Otherwise, David McKinley looked like he had a salami sliding down the side of his leg.

Megan Trammell was not the sort of woman to normally stare at a man's crotch. And especially not a young associate at her law firm. Sure, she, like any healthy, heterosexual women liked seeing handsome, well-put together men. And yes, of course, Meg would sometimes admire a man's well tended hair, groomed nails, perfectly shined shoes. She liked broad shoulders. And, yes, okay, sometimes, *in extremis* mind you, she might try to catch a glimpse of what promised to be a shapely ass.

David McKinley happened to have all of those things. Though his hair, wavy, dark, was a little longer than Meg usually liked, it worked on him. Somehow, he gave that slightly feminine feature a masculine tinge. He also had those eyes. Girls must lose themselves into those big, nearly black, luminous saucers, framed by long, thick, exquisite lashes. It wasn't the sort of thing men noticed, but it was the sort of thing women gushed over, much more so, indeed than a weird bulge in the crotch that had to be—*had to be*—an optical illusion.

Still, looking was harmless. Meg was married. Not just married, but *married*. Ten years. Three kids. A dog. Two cats. A house that literally had a white picket fence. She and Mal had the same friends, three couples, Tina and Max, George and Tammy, Ellen and Nico, who they saw in what had become almost a Viennese waltz of choreographed dinners at each other's places. They all had kids. The kids played together, more or less went to the same schools, played on the same soccer teams. The works. So it wasn't just that Meg and Mal, some ten years and three months ago, had said some words in a church. Rather that it sometimes seemed like every last bit of their lives was intertwined. Except for work, where, on occasion, Meg could look over a handsome man and have that experience just for herself.

She had to admit she'd been doing that a little too often with David. They not only worked together, but he was an associate in her group. He worked mostly with Richie Wong, but she sometimes gave David some assignments as well. The partners were expected to parcel out assignments to as many associates as possible, if for no other reason than to give them an opportunity to assess their work for when they came up for partnership.

Not that David was going to come up anytime soon. At twenty-seven, he was only in his second year at the firm, and anyway, Meg, thirty-five and a newly-minted partner herself, wouldn't be the decisive vote on any promotion decisions. But technically, she was one of his supervisors, and supervisors are not supposed to be checking out their subordinates, and especially not the possible optical illusion in a subordinate's crotch.

Worse yet, it seemed like David had noticed. She couldn't be sure. He hadn't said anything. But she was glancing in that direction, and then when she looked up, she saw him peek at her out of the corner of his eye as a quick, mischievous smile came across his face. *Busted*. Or maybe he was just checking her out? She blushed at that thought. Surely, she was too old for him to be interested. Rachel seemed more his type. She was an associate, Asian-American, tall, brilliant, with long, long, silky black hair, porcelain skin, and the longest legs Meg had seen outside a fashion show. Or maybe Kaylee the receptionist was more his speed. Blond, bubbly, big breasted, with large, blue eyes that make her look like a doll.

Surely David was not interested in Meg. Not thirty-five year old Meg, with her husband and three kids. Not Meg with her thick, long rust colored hair, so dense that she had to brush it out nightly to prevent it from turning into a tangled rat's nest. A redhead whose carpet didn't even match the drapes. She'd gotten so sick of disappointed boyfriends back in school that she'd actually gone ahead and shaved it all off, back before it was really *a thing*, which turned out to be a real turn on for guys, but also an issue. It made boys thinks she was sluttier than she really was…although, truth be told, it was worth noting that there *were* enough boys back then that, well, maybe the label wasn't so very far off.

But that was a long time ago, before pregnancy had broadened her hips and swelled her breasts. She was a tight little package back then. Now, no matter how much she worked out, she couldn't get her stomach from flat back to ripped, her ass from shapely back to hard. The cleavage was a nice benefit, especially in the summer when the sun tanned her upper chest, bringing out a wedge of freckles that seemed to encourage men to contort themselves to get a peek. Meg had always liked the attention. Probably something about being a late bloomer or having a distant father or something.

The tickler on her computer chirped at her, reminding her to log her time.

"Oh fuck," she groaned.

Another fifteen minute increment wasted on daydreams. At this rate, the mysterious optical illusion in David McKinley's pants was going to make her miss her monthly billable target.

*

"That's it. Right there. Hold it. Just like that." Mal couldn't take his eyes off her ass. It was tight without being small, like a ripe apple, and judging from the way her yoga pants stretched across it, she couldn't have been wearing anything under. He would have seen the lines.

Not that he should have been looking.

"Now I want you to stretch it out," he said, looking at the rest of the class. "Move back into down dog." The class of five women listened, transitioning out of their arm balances. "Good. Now down lower. Caterpillar. Good. Now all the way down."

Mal walked by his "students," although it was silly to think of them that way. One woman was in her fifties. Most were his age, mid-thirties.

He advanced the CD to the final meditation music and turned the lights low. "Now, everyone on their backs. Clear your minds. Let everything go."

He led them through the relaxation phase of the session. Inevitably, his eyes wandered. They were all in pretty good shape, but the young woman whose ass he'd been staring at was exceptional. She wore a gauzy, lavender tank top that didn't do much to hide her toned body. Her skin was milky white and unblemished, a striking contrast to her dark hair and even darker eyes—although thankfully those eyes remained closed.

He looked away as he felt his cock stir, and did his best to shake himself out of such unprofessional thoughts. He forced himself to think of other things. Healthier things—his wife, Meg, his kids, what to fix for dinner tonight.

Class ended. The women rolled up their yoga mats and filtered out. All of them but the young brunette. Seeing her linger sent a jolt through Mal, but he didn't let it show—he was a yoga instructor, masking emotion was usually easy.

She approached. She had an Eastern European look to her, and Mal half expected her to have an accent. When she spoke, though, it was crisp and American. "Thanks for today's session. You really pushed us."

"Did I? Sorry, I'm still trying to get the levels correct. *Yoga II* means something different for everyone."

"No, no. It was good. I like a challenge. I'd like to think I can keep up with anything you can dish out."

Mal dismissed the innuendo. He really needed to get his thoughts under control. "Well, I'm glad. You did well, too." The compliment just slipped out, and when those dark eyes flashed up at him, he wished he could have taken it back.

"I haven't taken a class with you before," she said. "I'm Elena."

"Mal."

They shook hands awkwardly. Mal turned and started packing up his bag when he realized that Elena hadn't left. He wondered if she was waiting for him to do something, so he started rambling. "I usually work at Body & Mind Yoga, but we have an agreement with this gym. We teach a class here every week. Usually, the owner, April, teaches the class, but she's on vacation now."

It was TMI, but this kind of thing usually happens when faced with a pretty girl—especially when a pretty girl looked at him the way Elena was.

"Body & Mind, huh? I'll have to check it out," she said.

Mal shouldered his bag and yoga mat. Elena walked out with him. "Do you teach a more advanced class?"

Mal was a good looking guy, and Elena wasn't the first girl to come on to him—they just normally weren't so striking. He usually shut these things down pretty quickly, but he let this one play out a little longer. Something about her friendly tone…or maybe her lovely ass.

"I do. Actually, I'm holding a handstand workshop in a couple of weeks."

Elena's eyes lit up, this time with genuine interest. "I'm terrible at handstands."

"They're tricky. A lot of it is confidence, though. We get so scared of falling that it paralyzes us. Self-fulfilling prophecy and all that."

They arrived at the main floor. Mal had a few administrative things to take care of in the offices. Elena was on her way out.

"Well, it was nice meeting you, Elena."

"Maybe I'll see you around," she replied in a way that seemed to make the *maybe* vanish into thin air.

She left with a backwards glance and a smile. Mal looked once last time at Elena's ass. It was a reminder that one of the main perks of being a yoga instructor was the existence of yoga pants.

"Yeah, man, it's a great view." The statement came with a clap on his shoulder. Mal turned to find one of the personal trainers at the gym grinning knowingly at him. "You've got a sweet gig, man. I thought I was lucky, but your clientele is like the cream of the crop."

Mal cleared his throat. This is where he was supposed to spout off something macho. "It's not bad," Mal said instead. "Rodney, right?"

"That's me," he nodded. He looked like a meathead, and the Jersey accent didn't help, but April, Mind & Body's owner, spoke highly of him. "You ever tap any of that?"

"Not in years. I ended up marrying one," Mal said. It was strange to think that his wife outside of the context of the last ten years of marriage, back when she was just 22, before the kids, before her career had taken off, before the life they'd built. Once upon a time, she'd been like Elena, just a nice ass in a pair of tight pants.

"That right there's your mistake, man," Rodney said. "Never marry them. That's not what we do."

The thought of Meg's dimpled smile brought one to Mal. "One day, maybe you'll meet someone who'll change your mind."

"Oh, I've met plenty of married chicks through this job. *Married* is my favorite type, too, if you know what I mean. They're all about discretion."

"I'll make sure my wife never visits this gym," Mal said with a laugh.

"Or send her my way if you're looking to spice a marriage up. I've done that a few times, too," Rodney said. Mal wasn't sure if he was serious or not.

"I'll keep that in mind."

Rodney nodded. "And better, if you get a chance, definitely take a ride with that one. She looked like fun."

Mal excused himself into the office, where he signed out. As he did so, Rodney's crass observation stuck with him—not about taking a "ride" with Elena, but about his job. He did have a nice job. He'd never been quite like Rodney, but he had met his fair share of women through yoga—other teachers, friends with benefits, and yes, a client from time to time. Then he met Meg and was smitten.

But that wasn't the only perk. For the most part, it was stress-free—wouldn't be very New Agey to be a stressed out yoga instructor. It kept him in shape, too, he thought, checking himself out in the mirror on the way out. At close to forty, he was in much better shape than most of the guys he knew his age. He'd started losing his hair in his late twenties, so opted to shave it off. He'd inherited the rich tan thanks to his Persian father and the blue eyes of his American mother, and the exotic look had given him a lot of success in his bachelor years.

On his way out, he ran into Tammy, one of Meg's best friends, and the wife of one of his best friends, George.

"Hey, Tam. How's it going?"

Tammy jumped a little when she saw Mal. "Hey, Mal, what are you doing here?"

"I was teaching a class. You should have joined."

Tammy seemed to relax. Mal had always thought that she was pretty—long, straight blond hair that suited her slender body and delicate beauty. But she was as close as family, so had kept the attraction to himself.

"How about you?" he asked.

"Me?" Tammy asked. "Oh, why am I here?" Tammy's laugh was as sweet as the rest of her. "Trying to get back in shape."

Mal glanced along her body, on display in a pair of cropped black pants and a tight racerback top. She didn't look like she needed the gym at all.

"Sorry, I need to run," Tammy said. "I've got an appointment with my personal instructor."

Mal nodded, although something didn't quite sit well with him. "Well, see you around."

"You will." And with that, she walked into the gym, flashing her membership card in front of the reader.

Mal watched her long enough to see her walk up to Rodney, who was leaning against the desk, waiting for her. Mal's stomach squirmed as he watched Rodney grin and nod at Tammy. As they disappeared into the gym, he didn't miss the way Rodney had his hand on Tammy's lower back. Rodney's comment haunted him:

Married is my favorite type, too, if you know what I mean. They're all about discretion.

Mal shook his head. He was just jumping to conclusions. Tammy loved George. They'd been together as long as he and Meg. They had as full a life as Mal's.

They're all about discretion.

Troubled, Mal hurried home.

Two

Home is where the heart is. It is also where the dishes and laundry are. The cooking, the cleaning, mowing the grass, picking up the dog poo, and, of course, the kids. The apple of one's eye. The little creature who in many ways do give life meaning, none of which prevents one from daily fantasizing about the day when you finally pack the last one of them off to college and are done with them.

In a way, Meg was grateful they'd started young. Justin was ten! Double digits. Angela eight, going on fifteen, and already was a handful. Even "the baby"—they still sometimes called him that— Darryl was six, and finally in school for a full day after a year of half-day kindergarten. Even though she was older than Meg, Ellen was talking about having another! Even Tammy had mentioned it once or twice, although Meg was pretty sure that Tam wouldn't risk her physique yet again. That girl already spent more time in the gym than was healthy for her. And at work, it seemed like all of her female colleagues had waited longer. It had surely made climbing the career ladder easier, but Meg was pretty sure she'd have the last laugh. After all, she'd gotten her cake and ate it too—family and career. She was a role model. And exhausted and often tetchy and well, frankly, miserable too often for comfort.

But that too shall pass, she reminded herself. They were over the hump. It was all going to be so much easier from here on out. It had better be. Another ten years like the last ten and she'd be dead. Or wishing for it. Whichever came first.

Mal was both her rock and the bane of her existence. The rock because with his flexible schedule he did more than his share of the childcare and housework. He picked up the kids at school. He did the grocery shopping. He ironed and folded the laundry. The bane because he was just *so fucking mellow.* It's what had attracted her to him. Well, that and his rock-hard body, and those eyes, heaven-sent panty-droppers. He still had that amazing body. And was still that no-stress, good-natured hippy, which sometimes drove Meg right up the fucking wall, because when you're anxious, stressed, nervous, it can be infuriating to have a spouse who just doesn't seem to share the same sense of *urgency* about things.

"License and registration, please."

Meg looked up at the rather frightening-looking county sheriff outside her car window. In the movies, "the sheriff" is usually fat and comic relief. This guy was neither. Well over six feet tall, with bulging biceps, and a buzz cut peeking out from under his oversized trooper hat, he was intimidating as all hell. She knew the problem. Her plates were out of date. Mal has promised to take care of it. She checked herself. He'd actually said he'd *try* to take care of it. Even though she was the lawyer, Mal could be maddeningly precise when it came to that sort of thing.

"I'm really sorry, sir," she said earnestly. "I'll take care of it right away."

He harumphed and continued jotting down on his notepad, leaving Meg with the choice of looking straight ahead out the windshield on turning her head in his direct and staring at his crotch. She decided to take a peek. After all, she was becoming quite an expert in crotch-watching.

She took in his gun belt, the ominous, cold metal of his semi-automatic, the canister of mace, the bright chrome of his handcuffs. That gave her a little jolt. Back before Mal, there'd been this guy, Robby. They'd dated for a while. He seemed like a nice guy. Well, he *was* a nice guy, but maybe a little kinky it turned out. He'd pulled out a pair of handcuffs one night...and Meg had freaked out. Ruined the mood and they broke up soon after. But months after, she had wondered about it.... And now with Officer Hardass....

It would serve Mal right. After all, he had promised, sort of, to take care of it. And he hadn't. So now, he could hardly complain if his wife had no choice but to do what this scary lawman demanded.

You'll need to come with me, miss.

And when she stepped out of the car. *I'll need to cuff you.*

Her arms behind her back. The cold, hard metal tight on her wrists. His strong hand gripping her by the upper arm, leading her away from the road, into the trees.

You can't just pretend the law doesn't apply to you.

I'm sorry, sir. Please, I'll....

...do anything. He'd say. *I know.*

He'd push her down. Her knees digging into the soft, mossy ground. Looking up at this powerful, frightening man. Watch him, slowly, deliberately unfasten his belt and lower it to the ground. Then the button on his slacks. Slowly pulling down his zipper. Extracting his thick, hard....

"Ma'am? Ma'am?"

"Huh? Oh yes," Meg replied, blushing furiously.

"Okay, I'll let you off with a warning, but get that taken care of," he said with a drawl and a smile.

He handed back her paperwork and strode back to his car.

Meg wiped her mouth with the back of her hand. But worse than the drool on her lips was the realization, unmistakable now that she focused on it, that her panties were suddenly quite damp.

"Oh God, what the fuck was *that*?" she whispered quietly to herself.

*

Meg walked in the front door to...bedlam. Mal chased Justin who chased Darryl who was chasing Rexi, their athletic yellow lab, who was holding what looked like a partially cooked chicken breast in her mouth. Angela stood on the sofa, cross-armed, practicing her *I'm am not amused* glare. Rexi took advantage of the open door to hurl herself outside, where she promptly disappeared into the back-yard pursued fruitlessly by the two boys. Angela followed after, still scowling, but unwilling to be left out of the action.

"Well, there goes dinner," Mal said. *He,* in contrast to Angela, did seem amused. "Welcome home!" He kissed his wife on the cheek.

"How'd that happen?" Meg asked.

"Darryl wanted to flip 'em, and...."

"You let our six year old play with the grill?"

"I was watching him."

She shook her head. Presumably the dog hadn't gotten all of the chicken.

"I got pulled over."

Mal gave her an apologetic shrug. "Sorry babe. I didn't get a chance. But hey, keep the ticket. If you get pulled over again—"

"He let me off with a warning."

Mal gave her a smirk. "Flashed him a little titty, eh?"

A silly game they played. Though he was the one who made his living with his body and she with her brains, Mal always liked to tease his wife that she got ahead mostly by being sexy. Meg always took it for what it was, an inside joke that also served to reassure her that he still found her attractive, no matter how many spandex-clad women he rubbed elbows with all day.

"Oh, I did more than that, *babe*," she replied. "I'd show you, but I'm sure the kids will be back soon."

His eyes flashed. Those gorgeous, soul-melting eyes. She felt another flutter of excitement.

"Oh, I doubt it. They'll never catch up to Rexi back there."

He stepped in closer. Meg was tempted to share the little fantasy about her and the police officer, even if as she tried to formulate the words it sounded more than a little rapey and creepy and yet still hot. She thought maybe even demonstrating for him, wrists crossed behind her back. She knew Mal would be both shocked and delighted. It had been years since she'd been able to treat him to a spontaneous hummer. But before she could even tease her husband further, a yellow blur shot past them, followed by three screaming and now muddy children.

Meg groaned in frustration. Mal, as usual, smiled and chased after the howling mob to corral them. Maybe tonight, she thought for a moment, though she knew that even if they were still in the mood by then, it would be their usual, perfectly pleasurable lovemaking beneath the covers, both too tired to even think of playacting out a new fantasy.

*

Despite the chaos of the evening, Mal felt charged. He'd decided that he was going to get lucky even before Meg got home. His class and thoughts of Elena had something to do with it, but it had also been nearly a week since they'd had sex. When Meg got home looking all frazzled and sexy, he couldn't stop thinking of *later*.

Today, she wore what Mal considered one of her sexy power suits, although what Meg claimed it was industry standard. He questioned how heels as tall as hers could be considered industry standard—but she kept wearing them, no matter how much she complained. Mal had been with Meg long enough to know that he knew it had to do with instilling confidence in her professional life, but also knew her well enough not to say as much. Whatever the reason, though, while her suit was neither incredibly short nor low cut, it was snug, and snug on a woman with Meg's curves was inevitably sexy.

Layered on top of that was her little story about the ticket. He knew that she was just teasing him, but the fact that she was teasing him at all was something new. It reminded him of a younger, sexier version of his wife—the Meg who'd once given him a blow job as he drove them back from a date, who used to keep her pussy shaved bare.

Not that she wasn't sexy now. He was reminded of that very acutely when he walked in on her stripping out of her sexy power-suit at night's end—they'd been so busy corralling the kids that she hadn't had a chance to change until now.

She stripped out of the blouse, revealing a beige bra—sensible except for the way it was fringed in lace. Mal watched from the bedroom door, quiet enough not to reveal himself. She shimmied out of the skirt, taking her panties with it—efficient as ever.

For the first time in what felt like forever, he looked at her and didn't see the woman he'd been married to for over a decade. He saw her as the sexy, vibrant woman that she was. She had a body just as good as most of the women who came to his yoga class. She'd developed curves with the kids, but wore them well.

Watching her kneel down to retrieve her pajamas confirmed just how well she wore them. She'd unpinned her hair, pulling the dark red and unruly locks into a messy ponytail that made her look even more ravishing. Or ravished.

Again, her story returned—the officer pulling her over and her suggestive story about how she'd gotten out of it. That triggered another memory, of the trainer, Rodney, and his comment about sending his wife to him.

He advanced before he could get deeper into those thoughts—uncomfortable ones that made him as uneasy as he was aroused. He snuffed them out as he pulled his shirt off.

Meg jumped, noticing him there for the first time. "Oh, hey."

"Hey, yourself," he said. He turned her around and kissed her. Her pajamas fell to the ground, forgotten, as she returned the kiss. He wanted to continue the conversation from earlier, about the officer, about what she pretended to do, but he couldn't seem to bring himself to go there. Instead, he kept on kissing, moving them to the bed.

Meg wanted to bring them back to the conversation, too, although like her husband, she hesitated. Instead, she watched him strip out of his pants, revealing the rest of his lean, muscular body. His cock was hard. Ready for her.

Mal crawled onto the bed, kissing her hotly. His fingers moved between her legs, finding her already wet. He wondered what had excited her, and the wonder in turn excited him. He kissed down her body, sucking her nipples to hard points before finishing between her thighs. He found her clit under her thatch of thick, dark curls. He pressed his tongue home, his lips chafing. He remembered a time when she shaved. Did Elena shave? Guilt flooded him as he thought of the hot, young brunette.

Meg bucked under the oral assault, her hand caressing Mal's shaved head as he ate her. He was so good at that, the man could teach a class. But right now, she needed more than a good licking. She needed cock.

"Get up here, baby. I need you."

Mal didn't need to be asked twice. He moved back over her, stretching his hard body over her as he pressed against her pussy. She took hold of it, guiding it inside.

"Yes!" she sighed.

"You feel so good," Mal groaned.

"So do you."

The officer slipped into her mind for a split second before she banished him. Only in his place, David McKinley appeared. David with his bulge. David with his pretty boy good looks. This time, she didn't fight the fantasy. She wrapped her legs around Mal's back, raked her fingers through her thick hair, and dreamed of David filling her. It set her body on fire.

Mal felt Meg's body language change, too, but was too busy thinking of Elena to notice. Elena and her tight ass. Elena and her dark eyes. Elena and her twenty-something body, sweet on the outside, but dirty beneath, Rodney encouraging him to take a ride.

"Yes, fuck me," Meg moaned. Her voice was thick. Husky. His imagination twisted. Elena became Meg. Mal became Rodney. And Rodney had his wife bent over a weight bench, his cock buried inside her, his thumb in her ass.

Meg cried out, fighting to muffle the sharp orgasm. Once again, the vision changed. Tammy took Meg's place, her lean body, her long, blond hair, pale and covered in sweat as Rodney fucked her.

He opened his eyes, banishing the lurid thoughts. Below him, Meg was in another world, her eyes shut tightly, sweat gathering on her brow. She was close. He rolled with her, shifting his cock inside her just the way he knew she liked. She opened her mouth in a silent moan. He thrust again, pushing her over the edge.

She came quietly, trained after all these years of having kids in the house. Mal pumped her a few more times, summoning Elena to help push him over the edge. Yes, he decided, Elena definitely shaved. Or waxed. And she probably took it up her sweet ass, too, something even a young Meg had never offered.

He collapsed beside her, their heavy breathing filling the abrupt silence. Mal's hand found Meg's. "I love you, honey."

"I love you, too. That was great." It wasn't the wild sex she'd had in mind earlier, but it was still thrilling. David McKinley and his large cock lingered in the aftermath before she washed him away by kissing her husband. "That was the perfect end to today."

"We should do this more often," Mal said.

"We should."

They cuddled as sleep descended, both knowing that tomorrow would probably bring just a little more routine. In those last moments before sleep, Mal thought about telling Meg about Tammy and his suspicions, but decided against it at last. He had only a hunch, no evidence, and Tam was so close to his wife. No sense rocking that boat until he knew more.

Three

You've got to be kidding me. As Meg walked into the office, there was David, suit jacket off, sleeves rolled up, squatting down to help one of the building maintenance guys push an old filing cabinet back onto a dolly. Man, he had a great ass. And the way his shirt was stretched across the expanse of his back, traps bulging with strain. Yum.

"Nice view, eh?" It was Susan Miller, the senior woman partner in the firm.

Susan was close to retirement age, but she still had a lewd sense of humor sometimes. Short and stocky, Susan was still from a generation when the choice was career or home. Meg knew she doted on her sister's kids and grandnieces and grandnephews, but she wondered if she ever regretted her choices.

Meg startled but then smiled. "If we caught two male partners eyeing one of our pretty, young, female associates, we'd turn and report them to HR," Meg noted.

"Probably," Susan replied. "But that's because they wouldn't stop at ogling, whereas we're just looking."

Speak for yourself, Meg thought, but then she looked over at the older woman's smile and realized that she'd been speaking ironically as well.

They shared a small, private laugh and then Meg continued on to her office.

Meg was swamped. So much so that she almost decided to forego her lunch workout to catch up. But as with every time that thought crossed her mind, she fought it off by imagining Mal surrounded by his spandex-clad acolytes, which was always enough to give her the motivation to hit the stairmaster regardless of the number of unreads in her email in-box.

*

The Sport and Health had all the aerobic machines in one big room, all facing a large wall of TVs. The step machines were in the back rows along with the ellipticals, followed by the various stationary bikes, and finally two rows of treadmills. It made it hard to watch the TVs, what with dozens of bouncing, pedaling, and running people in between, but that was fine with Meg. After a few minutes, she had trouble focusing on anything other than her misery and the pain in her thighs.

She closed her eyes and focused on the burn. Mal was always saying that Yoga worked just as well, and certainly his body supported the claim, but Meg had always needed that burn, that sweat, a racing heartbeat to reassure her that she was, indeed, doing all she could to keep it together.

When she opened her eyes again, she was startled to see David poised on the stationary bike in front of her. She'd never actually seen him at the gym, though she'd heard him talking about a class in the morning before work. He was on one of those individual spinning bikes, and she guessed that he was using it *in lieu* of his usual group class. Maybe something had come up this morning.

Or maybe, she thought wickedly, he got lucky last night and was sleeping in. Come to think of it, Kaylee was looking a little peaked this morning. Unbidden, the image of the little blonde on her knees sucking David's huge prick appeared in her mind. And then as David began pedaling faster and faster, ultimately rising out of his seat, she couldn't help but imagine him between Kaylee's legs, pounding away, his gorgeous, muscular ass clenching over and over as he drove the young woman to one climax after another.

Beep, beep, beep. Meg looked down to see that she'd reached her goal. David was still hammering away, and she was tempted to continue her workout just to continue watching, but the burn in her thighs convinced her otherwise. Anyway, it was best if she didn't. She'd had her fun and games with David these last few days, but now it was time to get him out of her mind. She was a partner after all.

*

Mal was setting up the room at Body & Mind Yoga when he looked up and saw Elena walk in and put down her mat. *Uh oh*, he thought. Instead of yoga pants and a long-sleeve shirt, she was in tight, little, gym shorts and a sports bra. It wasn't inappropriate, *per se*, but it was a little unusual and it put him a little on edge. That said, she easily pulled it off. Her ass was not the only thing hard about her, her abs were epic as well. He thought about bringing home a picture of the young hottie to show Meg that Yoga could sculpt a woman's body too. *Uh, no, that's not a good idea.*

Elena caught his gaze and strode up to him.

"Hi Mal. I hope you don't mind me coming here today."

He smiled. "Of course not. Good to see you."

"I definitely want to take that handstand workshop, so I figured I'd need to step up my game to get ready. You will get me ready, won't you?"

She was talking about fitness…or was she? Either way, he couldn't help but think about other ways he might get her ready, imagining his tongue flicking at her little clit, sucking on her shaved snatch…because in those shorts, it was pretty damn obvious she was fully shaved.

"Sounds good," he replied.

He forced a smile and hoped it didn't come off as lecherous, though he wasn't sure she'd mind if it was. Unless he was completely losing his mind, she was definitely coming on to him. He got a little thrill out of the notion that Rodney, that meathead, hadn't been able to get her, though he'd surely tried, that instead she was seeking *him* out. If he wasn't married….

He stopped himself. Not a healthy line of thought.

A few other women filtered into the room.

"Why don't you set up your mat and start your stretches, we'll start soon," he said.

She smiled. "*Anything* you say."

She wheeled and walked to a spot in the center of the room. Damn, she was out of this world. If he wasn't married, he'd definitely do all sort of filthy, disgusting things to her. And she seemed like that kind of girl who'd like it, who'd not only let you come on her face, but would then wipe it off with her fingers and lick them clean. He shuddered. No, definitely not a healthy line of thought.

*

Meg gasped. Oh God, she was so close, so close. Just a little bit more. Oh yeah, right there. Right there.

The hot water was raining down on her soapy, naked body. She was yanking on her stiff nipple, lifting her heavy, teardrop breast away from her chest. Two fingers pumped vigorously into her swollen cunt. Meg didn't usually masturbate this roughly, but as she imagined David taking her, pounding his prick inside her she couldn't help herself.

On her desk, legs spread wide, that handsome young man, with the mop of wavy hair, great ass and huge cock plunging into her again and again and again.

She came with another gasp, and grabbed the shower head to keep from collapsing on the wet tiles. As her tunnel vision eased, she could hear the voices around her of other women in the neighboring shower stalls.

Oh God, I just masturbated in a gym shower.

She shook her head.

Well, at least that should keep me from thinking about him this afternoon.

But it didn't.

Four

The following weeks progressed just like that for the both of them. Elena didn't attend all of Mal's classes, but enough that he began looking forward to her tight body and suggestive smile. David didn't always work out during lunch, but he started showing up more frequently. For Meg, just the off-chance that David would be there was motivation enough for her to never miss a workout.

A couple weeks after the first time she spotted him, she saw him working the bike when she emerged from the locker room. As usual, her heart fluttered as she checked out his lean body and cute ass. He had great calves, thick and powerful.

Without realizing what she was doing, she took the cycle machine right beside him. Her pulse rose. Her nipples tightened. She took a long, silent breath, but it didn't do much to calm that nervous buzz racing through her.

He didn't see her at first, so focused on the monitor in front of him. Meg smiled to herself, calmed a little by the anonymity.

Then he noticed her and the heat and tightness flooded back. "Oh, Meg. Hey."

She didn't miss the way his eyes flicked across her body. A wave of self-consciousness passed through her. Her outfit was new, purchased specifically to show off to David. The racerback tank scooped low enough to give an eyeful of cleavage, and the shorts, while not tiny, were small enough to put her sculpted thighs on display—thighs she'd worked hard for and wanted to show off.

David's sweep took it all in, lingering for the briefest moment in her cleavage. That sent a rush through her.

"Hey, I noticed you're coming here more during lunch," she said, seeking small talk.

"Yeah, the class I was taking in the morning changed teachers."

"Not as good?" she asked.

"No. She didn't push us enough."

"You like being pushed?" Meg couldn't believe the flirty question emerged from her mouth. She'd thought it, but hadn't intended to say it.

David held her eyes for a second before answering. "With the right...instructor, I love to be pushed."

Meg's face went red, but she didn't look away. She just smiled, managed to roll her eyes, and said, "I'll keep that in mind."

They both laughed before returning to their respective workouts. Meg cranked the resistance up, hoping to burn off some of her pent-up sexual energy. It didn't work. Not with David groaning beside her, the smell of his sweat and exertion curiously exciting.

She sighed. She needed to talk to someone about her obsession with this guy. Not Mal. That wouldn't go down well. But part of the reason she was so pent up was because she'd held it all inside. So maybe... Tammy. Of all her friends, she figured Tam would understand. She made a note to call her later that day.

*

At the same time, out in the suburbs at Health and Fitness, Mal was leading a gym class through its final relaxation exercises. It was a small group, just as they usually were at the gym. Elena wasn't there, which was both a relief and a disappointment, but there was plenty of eye-candy. The stay-at-home moms out here took physical fitness as seriously as if it were written into their job descriptions.

He thought of Meg, who managed to maintain her body even with a job. He was proud of her. That wasn't an easy thing to do, and while he'd always subscribed to a more measured approach, like Yoga, he couldn't deny that those driving sessions on the aerobics machines were effective. She seemed more focused on those lunches than ever, and the results were evident in the last few weeks.

"Alright, class, I'll see you next week," he said as they filtered out.

This gym in the suburbs was far less crowded than the one Megan was at in the city. Here, things got crowded after work and on the weekends, which is why Mal would never teach a class here during prime time.

He packed up his things and decided to hit the shower. He normally took one at home, but he was meeting a friend for a late lunch, so figured he'd go straight from here.

In the shower, his thoughts inevitably drifted to Elena. He wondered what she did for a living. She didn't appear to be married, but frequently attended his weekday classes. He wouldn't be surprised if she was a model, he figured. She was young enough, and certainly pretty enough. Or maybe she was a stripper. That sent a surge through his soapy cock.

What are you doing, man? he thought to himself. *You're not going to beat off in the gym's shower, are you?*

He groaned, stepped under the spray, and rinsed off.

Dried and dressed, he felt great. One of the things he enjoyed so much about teaching Yoga was how good it made him feel. He did the same exercises that they did—when he wasn't walking around, correcting—so by the end of a class, he was loose and ready to take on anything.

He signed out, said goodbye to the few folks he knew working there, then realized that he'd forgotten his yoga mat up in the exercise room. Groaning, he turned around, climbed the stairs and entered the now quiet upstairs, where the classes were. At this hour, the gym had nothing scheduled, and he just hoped that they kept the rooms unlocked.

The room was dark, but wasn't locked. He entered, retrieved his bag from the far side of the room, and heard it. A moan. He was pretty sure of it. That, or someone was playing some pretty interesting music in one of the other exercise rooms.

"Uh, fuck!" A woman's cry, unmistakable. That wasn't music.

Mal grinned to himself. Someone was having the kind of fun that he wished he could have. The room that they were in was actually the first half of a larger room, separated by a partition. The fucking couple must have been in the other half of the room.

"Oh, Rod. Oh, Rod!"

"Shh. Keep it quiet, you little slut."

Mal's grin widened. Oh course it was Rodney behind this. He started to leave when he noticed that one of the partitions hadn't been fully closed. In the dark of his room, light leaked in. Drawn to the slice of light, Mal assured himself that he'd just look to confirm his suspicions. If only he'd resisted and walked away....

Sure enough, it was Rodney drilling his hips into a blonde that he had bent over the ballet bar. She had a trim body that bordered on too skinny, and long straight golden hair that fell around her face, obscuring it from view. She clutched the bar with both hands as Rodney bounced her along his cock.

"Couldn't wait for our usual time, could you, slut?" Rodney said.

"No. I needed it sooner—"

"Can't get my cock out of your mind, that it?"

"No. I mean, yes. Uh—yes!"

Mal's ears perked up. There was something familiar about her voice. He looked again. The blonde still wore her sneakers and socks, but now that he was looking, he saw it—the petals of a rose tattoo on her ankle, barely obscured. Still, plenty of women had rose tattoos there.

"Ready for Friday night?" He pressed a thumb against her asshole. "Ready to try something completely new?"

The blonde threw her head back as she crested. Her hair fell away, her face was clearly reflected in the mirror. It was Tammy, George's wife, Meg's best friend. Mal reeled in horror. No. No, it couldn't be! But it sure as fuck was.

Rodney pulled his cock out of her, grabbed her by her shoulders, and spun her around. Tammy moved efficiently. They'd done this before. She dropped to her knees, grabbed Rodney's sizable cock, and sucked it into her mouth. He came a moment later, and Mal couldn't stop watching. He was drawn between the way her throat moved as she swallowed his come, and the blur of her fingers on her clit.

Her naked body was as sweet as he'd always imagined. Her tits looked bigger than he'd suspected, but were still smaller than his wife's. She had a light brown landing strip above her clit, neat and tidy, and glistening wet. She seemed to come again before she was done swallowing Rodney's seed.

Mal came to his senses, pulling back and getting his things together before he was caught. He occupied his mind with anything and everything that didn't have to do with the revelation he'd just had—that one of his best friends was cheating on another of his best friends.

Instead, he thought about how he was sweaty beneath his clothes. He'd need another shower, but that would have to wait. His friend was probably already at the restaurant. He'd have to call ahead.

Shouldering the yoga mat and his bag, he got the hell out of there.

*

"You sure nothing's wrong?" Nick asked for perhaps the half-dozenth time.

Mal forced a smile. "I don't know, maybe I'm coming down with something."

Nick laughed. "I thought you yogi types never got sick. Always have your energy in harmony."

"Fuck you," Mal replied, but with a smile. But even still he felt the need to give some response, even if he wasn't going to mention what he was really thinking about. "Just things are a little hectic right now, Meg's working a ton, the kids are, um, going through a high-energy phase, I'm juggling slots at two different clubs. You know, the usual."

Mal was a little surprised at his own words. He'd been planning to just deflect Nick's questioning, but instead had unleashed a torrent that even as he was saying it resonated surprisingly deeply.

Nick nodded sympathetically. "See, and that's why I'm never going to get married."

Mal rolled his eyes. *It could be worse. He could be George. At least Meg wasn't fucking around on him. Or....*

None of that was any of Nick's business though. "Yeah, that's why."

Nick laughed. "Well that and my general misogyny and raging alcoholism."

"Precisely."

Mal's feeling of unease, of being out of sorts, didn't end with lunch. He carried it all through the afternoon, a pit in his stomach. Him and Meg, Tammy and George, Tina and Max, Ellen and Nico… just because they were all friends and at roughly the same life stage it didn't mean that their relationships were identical.

Yet, it was very disconcerting to think that Tammy was cheating on George. Did Meg know? She had to. She and Tammy were super close. Why wouldn't Meg tell him? Did she have her own secrets she was hiding as well? He'd never suspected his wife before, but this all made him very uneasy…and also weirdly excited. He wasn't turned on, not quite, or maybe he was, though he didn't want to admit it. But he couldn't help making that jump, from Tammy's demonstrated infidelity to the possibility of his wife's own misbehavior.

All through the rest of the day he'd planned to talk to Meg about what he'd seen at the first available moment. But then, in bed, with the kids down, and just a few minutes before they turned out the lights, he chickened out. It suddenly seemed weird to discuss it. Or maybe he was frightened of the conversation that might ensue, the revelation he'd hear. Also, in a weird way, he sort of liked the ambiguity of the situation. There was something of a thrill in suspecting his wife, at the very least of being complicit in covering up her friend's affair, but also wondering what else she was keeping from him.

*

Meg was up early, a blizzard of work had just come in and she wanted to get an early start. She showered quickly and peered into her closet. They were behind on laundry. Mal would surely fold the laundry and bring it up from the basement in his own good time, but right now, Meg was out of underwear. Well, not completely out. Just out of the normal stuff. What she did have, still in her closet, was the racy stuff, the lingerie she broke out on those date nights or weekends away with Mal, when she knew he'd have the time to properly appreciate it. But, right now, she was desperate, so underwear was underwear.

The set she chose was Mal's favorite, just a bra and panties set, but the bra was a lacy, black demi-cup that barely contained her full breasts, and the matching panties were also skimpy, gauzy in the front and tapered to a narrow thong in the back. She checked herself out in the mirror. Very sexy. Also very unprofessional. She wondered what David would think if he knew what she was wearing under her suit. She felt a flutter in her stomach, even as her mind scolded her. *Well, he's not going to find out, now is he?*

She finished dressing. A grey pencil skirt and a snug, cotton pullover. Another glance in the mirror. There, perfectly respectable. The outfit was a little tight, but with the skirt ending below her knee and the shirt covering up her cleavage, no one would think anything of it. What she wore beneath would be her little secret. And maybe tonight, Mal would have the opportunity to properly unwrap her.

But her fantasies wouldn't wait until tonight. Sitting in her car, the scratchy roughness of the lace against her breasts, the sensation of the thong wedged firmly between her cheeks, drew her attention again and again. She tried to focus her thoughts on Mal, sexy, sexy Mal, stripping her, pulling aside the fabric of her thong so he could tongue her juicy slit, but David kept intruding on her thoughts. *Mal eating me out…. David thrusting hard inside me.* Her hand drifted down between her thighs.

HONK! She swerved to the right, back into her own lane. Her heart raced. *Fuck that was close.* Now that would be a fun conversation. *What happened honey? Oh nothing, I was just jerking off thinking about a co-worker when I sideswiped a Porsche SUV. The usual.*

The near accident cleared her mind temporarily and she made it to work without incident. She even managed to sneak into her office without running into David doing something athletic or sexy. But before she could get to work, there was a quiet knock on her door.

Meg looked up and was startled to see David, looking haggard, a little rumpled, and oddly enough even sexier for it. The office was almost empty. No one at all on down on this side of the floor yet. No one would even know if she invited him into her office and....

"You're getting an early start," he said amiably.

She nodded and smiled, buying a little time to calm herself. "Yeah, yeah, lots of work."

"Oh, I don't mean to bother you then...."

"No, no problem, come on in." *Oh God*, why had she just said that? Surely it would have been better to let him leave, deal with him later, when there were more people around, and she was feeling less, um, wound up.

He really did look tired. "Have you been here all night?" she asked.

He nodded sadly. "Yeah, discovery. We have like a million documents to go through. That's what I'm here about actually."

She nodded sympathetically. "I know it's tedious, but it has to be done. People always talk about automating it, but that would be a mixed blessing, especially for younger associates. We all went through it."

"Oh, I know. I'm not complaining. I get it's a rite of passage. It's just...that's pretty much all Richie has available."

"Yeah, his matters are paper heavy."

"So," David continued, "I was wondering if, you know, you needed any help on the Anderson matter."

Meg smiled. A law school classmate who did entertainment law had referred the case to Meg after getting conflicted out. Simple breach of contract case. Young Melanie Anderson, former Nickelodeon star, now best known for getting caught not once, not twice, but three times flashing her bare snatch at paparazzi when getting out of cars, was being sued by her studio for parasailing in Acapulco. Her contract had a "no skydiving" clause, and since a parachute was also in use here, it was a convenient way to dump a "star" whose main interest now seemed clubbing anyway. Meg would be arguing the case before an arbitrator in LA at some point.

"Looking to add a little glamour to your life?"

He grinned. "I also think she could use a good man in her life."

Meg laughed. Melanie seemed to have no shortage of men in her life, though indeed their quality seemed to be lacking. "Ah, so cute, you're going to rescue her."

He shrugged. "Never mind. It was just a silly idea."

Meg was working it through her mind. There wasn't a lot of work on this case, though she *could* use some help on tracking down some details on the ground.

"There would be some travelling," she cautioned.

"That'd be the best part," he replied.

She felt a flutter in her stomach. She knew *he* meant going out to LA, maybe meeting Melanie, but *Meg's* imagination immediately went to David and her traveling together, sharing meals, staying in the same hotel…. A very, very bad idea.

"I'll talk to Richie about it. See if he can do without you for a bit."

David smiled brightly. "I'd really appreciate it." He stood. Oh God, that bulge again. Jesus. "I'll let you get back to work. Want the door open or shut?"

"Shut, please," Meg replied. Other people were starting to filter in and she needed quiet.

He shut the door and Meg squirmed in her seat. She glanced down and noticed that her nipples were poking through her pull-over—the one real downside of wearing a more sheer bra. David wasn't the only one showing off through his clothes.

She knew she was in dangerous territory. Her crush on David was growing day by day, and now she was potentially going to arrange it so they were working closer together still. She knew she should have said no. She still could. But she knew also she wouldn't because she liked the fantasy too much. She liked thinking about the two of them together, in business class, sipping champagne on the long transcontinental flight, sharing a cab back to the hotel, lunches, dinners, drinks after. Adjoining rooms, to make it easier to work of course, letting it build, build, build until that one night, she'd invite him in, and he'd take her, long and hard with that big cock of his, her hands clawing at his back, her nipples digging into his—*Ahhhh!*

Meg gasped for breath and removed her hand from her wet panties. *Very professional Meg.* She *knew* she had to say no to the Anderson matter.

She picked up the phone. Dialed.

"Hey Richie? Any chance you can give me some of David's hours for a bit later this month? I have a case out in Cali that I could use his help on.... Great, thank you."

She hung up the phone and stared at it, her hand again sliding between her damp thighs, higher and higher....

*

Mal had gotten the kids off to school without incident. Well, Justin had thrown a ball at Darryl, which went through the smaller boy's fingers, popped him in the face and then landed in a bowl of cereal splashing milk all over Angela, at which point Darryl had started to cry, Angela to shriek about her clothes being ruined and Justin to yell at Darryl that it was all his fault for being such a klutz, at which point Darryl threw applesauce at his older brother, and Rexi took advantage of the confusion to swipe raw bacon off the kitchen counter. So, all in all, a normal morning.

But once the kids were gone, the morning became anything but normal. Mal had had difficulty sleeping even with all his breathing and relaxation tricks. The image of Tammy getting fucked by Rodney kept replaying in his mind, and with it all those questions. Did his wife know? Did she have secrets of her own? And then other thoughts too. It wasn't all talk with Rodney. Of course, he knew trainers hooked up with clients. That was one of the perks of the job in a sense, but seeing it brought home again the reality of it, the reality that the thing with Elena didn't have to be just a little flirtation. It could easily, if he wanted it to, become the real thing. And damn, that would surely be a hell of a good time. Meg was gorgeous and passionate. But Elena promised *wild, raw, dirty*—shit that he could not—*would not*—do with his wife, the mother of his children.

He was still wrestling with those thoughts as he walked into the locker room to change. Rodney was standing in front of his locker, almost nude as he changed as well. The guy was an asshole, but he was really built. Mal had always been slender. He was more ripped than Rodney, but Rodney was bigger, more powerful. Mal had never been able to add muscle mass like that and was a little jealous.

"Yo man," Rodney acknowledged him.

Mal remembered back to Rod's encounter with Tammy. The way he'd teased her asshole and talked about Friday night. An idea formed in his mind.

"Got big plans this weekend?" Mal asked.

"Hitting up a club tomorrow, then we'll see, you know."

Would he really take Tammy to a club? Was she that reckless to be seen in public with him?

"Dance party really. Drop a little E. Everyone is hot and sweaty. Gets girls in the mood to do just about *anything*. You should come by, man. Bring that little slut Elena and get fucking crazy."

"Not sure about that. I'd probably bring my wife."

He laughed. "Cool. I'd like to check *her* out. You know how I feel about married women." Mal knew Rodney was busting his chops, but he felt a surge of jealousy anyway...and a little weird excitement. "Actually, you probably know the place. It's in the old crossfit facility that closed down on Tremont? Sort of cool, they put up all these lights and shit, but you still have a bunch of the fitness equipment, ladders, ropes, swings. Makes for a crazy scene."

Mal nodded. "Cool, maybe we'll check it out."

Rodney finished dressing and left. Mal sat and thought it through. He knew he'd never be able to just mention that Tammy was cheating...but if he and Meg happened to see her out with Rod... well, then that was something different. And this club sounded perfect. Meg would be suspicious if he suddenly mentioned some chic new club downtown, but this seemed right up his alley.

*

Meg had skydived once. Mal had wanted to try it, so she went with him. He'd loved it, of course. She'd been terrified. For the longest time, before the parachutes were pulled, they just fell. Wind in their faces, ground thousands of feet below, the world racing up at them, they fell. Meg hated that feeling. As exhilarating as it felt—and it certainly was exhilarating—it was out of control, and she was the kind of woman who preferred control.

That's exactly how she felt now, with David. She was falling and falling and falling, and couldn't quite bring herself to pull the parachute. Three times over the course of the day, she picked up the phone and almost called Richie, almost told him that she'd found someone else to help out on the Anderson case. She never made that call.

*

Mal planned to wait until the kids were asleep to broach the subject of Friday night. He'd done some research into the club Rodney had mentioned. It was easy to find based on Rodney's description—*Pumped*. True to his word, it had been a crossfit facility that had closed down. They'd left the gym's interior semi-intact. The whole thing was gimmicky as hell, but that didn't bother Mal. It had been ages since they'd gone out clubbing. It would be fun, even without the Tammy situation.

When Meg got home, frazzled, Mal picked a moment of calm in the chaos to follow her up to the bedroom as she changed out of her work outfit. She was just pushing her pencil knit skirt off when he walked in. Immediately, he froze. Her lingerie wasn't her usual, everyday wear.

"Sexy," he blurted.

Meg turned, smiling over her shoulder. "I thought you'd like it."

She had an ass designed for thongs—and luckily, since image was so important and her skirts were usually tight, she wore her fair share of them—but this particular thong had always been one of his favorites. The lacy frills were exciting, and the way the bra plunged did awesome things to her tits.

But he couldn't shake this niggling question of why was she wearing it? Maybe it was the whole Tammy thing, and Rodney's comment about wanting to meet his wife, but Mal's mind immediately wondered if she'd worn that lingerie for someone else.

"I do," he managed. As he crossed the room, for a brief moment, he imagined that he wasn't her husband, but someone else—another man checking out the way the thong plunged between her cheeks, the way her bra opened in the front, in the center of her deep cleavage.

Meg, watching him watch her, was having the exact same fantasy.

"Hi stranger," Mal said, collecting her in his arms. "You come around here often?"

Meg giggled. "Yes, but usually with more clothes."

"Shame." He kissed her, his hands moving down to her butt. "I could get used to this."

Meg nodded. "Me, too."

"MO-OM!" came the yell of a child downstairs.

The two sighed. "Well, to be continued."

Mal nodded. He started to leave, then paused. "Hey, I was wondering…. You doing anything Friday?"

"Nope," she said.

"Want to go out with me? There's this club that just opened on Tremont. Has kind of a gym/training theme to it. Sounds goofy, but some people at the gym were talking about it." It all came out in a rush, and he hoped he didn't sound as nervous as he felt.

Meg didn't say anything at first. She just blinked at looked at him. Then she laughed. "You want to go clubbing?"

"Yeah. Why not?" This was a problem he knew how to deal with. His charm let him get away with crazier ideas in the past. "It'll be fun. Like old times."

"What about the kids?"

"Babysitter."

"What about—"

"Stop overthinking it. The only thing you need to worry about is what to wear so that I can show you off."

Meg laughed. She'd given in, even if she didn't know it. "Oh, is that what this is all about, huh?"

"Isn't it always about that?" Mal kissed her.

"MO-OM!"

"We'll talk about this later," she said. Mal knew he had her.

Five

"*Pumped*. Really?" Meg asked as their cab dropped them off in front of the old gym.

"I know, points off for the cheesy name, but I've heard pretty good things about it," Mal said.

"Really? Because I've read that it's a meat market." She was mostly giving him a hard time, though she *had* read that. At least the crowd was mostly her age—late twenties into thirty.

"You selling?" Mal said with that infuriatingly charming grin of his. "You sure look packaged like you are."

Meg blushed. The way her husband looked at her felt like...well, it felt the way David sometimes looked at her at the gym. For a moment, Mal didn't look at her the way he had for years, but the way a stranger would, like a potential hookup. It was thrilling.

Was that what she thought of David? A potential hookup?

She shook her head. No, she wasn't going down that road. Not tonight. Tonight was about her and Mal and reconnecting.

They got out of the cab, ready for the evening. Meg smoothed her hands across her jeans, although they were tight enough that they'd rip before they'd wrinkle. She'd been proud that she still fit into it, although she worried that her blouse was too low cut. As she looked down the line, though, she realized it was almost modest in comparison. Inwardly, she admitted that she had some of the best cleavage on display—the store bought competition didn't count.

On the arm of a guy like Mal, the two of them earned more than their fair share of stares. He'd put on linen slacks and a dark blue button-up. The top two buttons were left undone, hinting at his toned upper body and the mat of dark chest hair—man-cleavage, she'd once joked to him. He looked hot as always.

The line wasn't terribly long, which was probably a bad thing for the longevity of this club, but most definitely a good thing for a couple used to going to bed around this time, rather than just beginning the night. When they stepped inside, though, and the sea of undulating humans opened up before them, Meg had to revise her pessimistic assessment.

It was dark, and the flashing lights made it nearly impossible for her eyes to adjust. Hip hop roared in her ears, its beat reverberating in her chest. She stepped into it, feeling her body sink into the sound.

A smile spread across her face, one she couldn't shake. Didn't want to. She was transported to her early twenties, before kids, before even Mal, back when she was single and the whole world was spread out before her. Back when everything presented the possibility of something new. Was that what she'd been missing? Was that why she'd been crushing on David McKinley?

"This is awesome!" Mal shouted into her ear. Shouted, because there wasn't a chance in hell that he'd be heard over the music.

Meg nodded. It was. He shouted something about getting a drink. She wanted to dance instead, but a drink sounded good, too. "Let's go."

*

Mal had to keep reminding himself why he was there—to catch Tammy with Rodney and point them out. He almost had to force himself to look away from his wife, who looked fucking amazing in her skin tight jeans and that sparkly, black top. Haltered, it served her tits up on a platter. She'd pinned her red hair up, put on more make-up than usual, and barely looked like herself. She looked like the kind of girl he thought Elena was—or the woman he'd first been attracted to, back when she was just a student.

He wasn't the only guy to notice, either. When they thought he wasn't looking—and sometimes when he was—they'd stare at her. They wanted her. He felt this confused swirl of jealousy and excitement around it. This place was filled with attractive women, and his wife measured up among the hottest.

At one point, as he was returning from the bathroom, Mal spotted a guy hitting on her at the bar. He was younger than Mal by about ten years, good looking in a cocky way—a Rodney way. Meg regarded him with controlled amusement. She wasn't buying his shit, but seemed to be having fun anyway.

He gestured to the dance floor, going as far as putting a hand on her arm. She didn't remove it, but didn't move, either. She shook her head, mouthed a *Sorry*, and held up her ring. That didn't seem to totally dissuade the guy, though, who seemed to say back, *Come on.*

A twisted side of Mal wanted to keep watching. This exchange was thrilling. Here was a glimpse of Meg when she was single. That smile. The confidence she had with this guy. Had she played him like that, Mal wondered? She'd certainly strung him along for quite some time before inviting him back to her place.

Then he pushed through the crowd, joining her flirtation with the guy. Meg didn't react like she'd been caught. Instead, she calmly turned to Mal and snuggled against him. "There you are, husband.

This is Marty. He was just leaving."

"Nice to meet you, Marty," Mal said.

Marty grumbled, but took the hint, moving on in search of something new.

"Was he bothering you?" Mal asked.

"Nothing I can't take care of myself."

Mal felt that rush again, like fresh air. Like something brand fucking new. "Maybe I should leave you alone more often."

"And what happens when I find something I like?" She was teasing him, he knew, but Mal's chest tightened anyway.

"Would you have fun if you did?" This was a conversation he wasn't sure that he wanted to have yet—a conversation not even fully formed.

She hesitated a fraction of a second before answering—but it was enough to send a shiver along Mal's spine. "Only if the guy was you."

Mal nodded, looking out across the crowd. On cue, he saw them—Rodney and Tammy, entwined in one another's arms on the dance floor. Tammy, like his wife, was barely recognizable as the suburban mom he regularly hung out with. She wore a skin-tight white dress that glowed in the black lights of the club. Her hair was pulled back in a long, high ponytail that flipped around her as she shimmied against Rodney, whose hands were all over her ass.

Mal's heart rate shot up. He took a deep breath. Here goes.

"Hey, that's not Tammy, is it?"

*

At first, Meg didn't believe it. She *couldn't* believe it. The blonde pressed against the young hardbody just looked like her best friend. There was no way that she actually was. "I don't...think so?"

Mal was studying her closely, gauging her reaction for some reason. "I think it is. Look again."

She didn't want to, but she did. At that moment, Tammy threw her head back and laughed at whatever the young guy had said. Yeah, that was definitely Tammy. Meg could practically hear her friend's hearty laugh. What the fuck?!

And then Tammy did something that defied all logic. She leaned in and kissed the guy. Hard. On the lips. With plenty of tongue.

Meg's mouth fell open. Everything around her went muted. She didn't see the swell of the crowd. She didn't hear the music. She didn't smell the mixture of sweat, booze, and perfume. All she could do was stare at Tammy as she traded spit with some guy who was definitely not George.

And deep down—so far down that she didn't want to even acknowledge it, she was excited for her friend. No, *excited* wasn't the right word. Envious felt closer.

"Shall we say hi?" Mal asked.

The scene returned with his voice—the club, the noise, the reality of it all.

"No!" she said instinctively. She felt embarrassed for Tammy at that moment. Felt this natural reflex to protect her friend. "I mean, I don't want to embarrass her or anything."

"Oh, come on. It'll be a blast."

Meg couldn't read her husband, but when he took her hand and led her out onto the dance floor, she didn't resist. This was insane. She felt this huge amount of anxiety well up inside her, for her friend. This was about to be a nightmare situation for Tammy—and shamefully, Meg could relate more than she wanted to. She thought of one of their friends catching her with David, the sensation of panic so real she nearly pulled away from Mal. She'd never let this happen.

Never.

But California is so far away from home, an evil, little voice reminded. She crushed it just as they arrived at Tammy, who hadn't see them approach, her back to them.

"Hey, man, how's it going?" Mal asked...the guy. Confused, Meg started to open her mouth when Mal went on. "Rodney, I'd like you to meet my wife, Meg. Meg, this is one of the guys I work with at the gym."

Tammy turned, although her reaction wasn't the panicked one either of them were expecting. "Mal. Meg! It's so good to see you."

She actually hugged a confused Meg. *What the hell was going on here?* she thought.

"You guys know each other?" Rodney grinned. If he was ashamed at being caught as a philanderer, he didn't show it, either. "Small world."

"Is George here?" Meg asked, trying to make sense of this crazy scene.

"Hope not," Tammy said with a giggle. That was when Meg noticed how dilated her eyes were.

"Tam, are you high?"

The blonde's eyes brightened. "Yes! You want a pill? Rod's generous like that."

Now things really felt nostalgic of her early twenties. She was no stranger to Ecstasy, although it wasn't her party drug of choice back in the day, mostly for the same reasons she didn't like skydiving. But she'd never admitted that aspect to Mal, mostly out of embarrassment.

"Um, I think I'll pass," she said. She glanced at Tammy. "Can I talk to you for a moment? Alone?"

"Sure! Excuse us, babe."

Meg practically pulled her friend out of there, leaving the two guys—who apparently knew each other—alone.

"What are you *doing*?!" She had to resist herself from shaking some sense into her friend.

"Same as you. Having fun," Tammy said.

Meg sighed. Tammy was rolling on E. She wasn't going to get much out of her. "Does George know you're here?"

"Nope."

"Come on, let's get you some water. You'll be getting thirsty really soon."

"That's so sweet of you, Meg. Have I told you how much I love you?"

Meg ignored her friend and got them to the bar, where she paid for a couple $4 bottles of water. "How long has this been going on?" she asked at last.

"A couple months now."

"Why? Are things bad between you and George?"

"No, not bad. Just...boring. Rodney, he's *not* boring." She giggled. "He's incredible. Meg, the things he does to me. The way he makes me feel.... I'm getting excited just thinking about it!"

Meg's stomach squirmed. She ignored it. "It's reckless, Tammy. You've got a family. You've got a life! Anyone could have seen the two of you tonight. You're lucky that it was me."

"I knew that you'd keep my secret," Tammy said with a smile. Then, out of nowhere, she leaned in, grabbed Meg, and kissed her—like really, really kissed her, tongue and everything.

"Tammy, what are you doing?" Meg said, pushing her friend away.

"I've always wanted to do that. Sorry." Her smile contradicted the apology. "You're so beautiful, Megan. Have I ever told you that?"

"Tammy, you're high. *Everything's* beautiful right now." She didn't say how the kiss left a tingling sensation inside her. She'd never been with a woman, never thought that was something she was into, but she had to admit that Tammy's lips felt good. "You need to get out of here before someone else sees you."

"Okay," Tammy said with a grin.

"I'm serious! I'll deal with Mal."

Tammy giggled. "I bet you will. Can I watch?"

"Come on," Meg said, dragging her friend back to the two guys.

They'd moved off the dance floor, over to a wall where small groups had gathered to set their drinks, tables made of CrossFit tires, chin-up bars on the walls, and climbing ropes dangling from the ceiling giving the place a kinky, bondage vibe. Rodney, Tammy's... lover—that word just sounded so wrong—was hot in a way that was totally Tammy's type. George had been like that once—fit, bulky, cocky. Meg could see the appeal, even if he wasn't exactly her type. She liked her men leaner, like Mal...and David. *No, no, no.* It was probably that kind of thinking that got Tammy mixed up with Rodney in the first place.

Meg interrupted whatever conversation the guys were having, addressing Rodney. "I don't know what your game is, but you need to get her out of here. She's got a family. She has friends all over the place. This could ruin her."

"Baby, I've *already* ruined her."

Meg rolled her eyes. "Spare me the cocky bullshit and take her home. Or back to your place, or whatever. She can't be seen like this."

"Feisty," Rodney said. "Want to join us?"

She looked to Mal to say something, but her husband watched it all silently. Damn him yet again! She ignored the question and addressed her friend. "Tammy, we'll talk tomorrow. Drink lots of water.

And be safe."

"Don't worry, Megan. We're always safe," Tammy said.

Meg blushed. She hadn't meant it like that. Too late, the couple left. Meg glanced at her husband. "You know that guy?"

"Yeah."

She was tipsy, but not enough to slow her down. "You knew they'd be here, didn't you?"

"No...not exactly."

"Liar!" She should have been angry, but it was hard to be angry at her husband.

"I didn't know how else to tell you. I figured that, you know, you had to see it for yourself."

"So you knew! How long?"

"Just a couple days. Seriously, I'm as shocked as you. And...."

"What?"

Mal shuffled.

"Spit it out, Malik!"

"I wasn't sure if you knew or not."

"I didn't!" Then: "What a sec. This was some kind of test?"

"Not exactly. I mean...no, not a test. I just thought this was the best way to clue you in."

Meg was shaking her head before he'd even finished talking. "We're leaving now."

"But we just got here."

"I don't feel like dancing anymore."

Mal sidled up to her, pulling her into his arms. "In the mood for something else?"

"Nope."

He kissed her neck, and goddamn it but she felt a tingling between her legs. "I saw you and Tammy kiss. That was unexpected."

"Was for me, too!" But his words had their intended effect. Her stomach fluttered.

"Makes me wonder what your Mom's Club meetings are really like."

Meg rolled her eyes, laughing. "Keep dreaming."

"I plan to," he whispered, kissing behind her ear. "Want to check out the bathrooms?"

Megan wasn't sure if he was serious. She chose to believe that he wasn't. "No, but we can continue this conversation in our bedroom."

"I like the way you think, Mrs. Trammel."

*

Except they weren't thinking exactly in the same way. As they left the club and proceeded down Tremont toward the Hilton to find a cab, Meg's heels click-clacking on the sidewalk was the only sound either of them made. And once in the taxi, with the driver inches away, Mal didn't have the courage to intrude on Meg's obviously foul mood.

They paid off their surprised babysitter, who was too worried about the obvious tension between her employers to rejoice at being paid a full night's worth of wages for just an hour of work.

Mal followed his wife in their bedroom, where without preamble she stripped out of her tight outfit. Had he misread her excitement for anger? Man, that idea was a turn-on, even more than the fact that she looked absolutely delectable in her skimpy bra and panties. Was it the idea of her friend cheating on her husband that had her so worked up? Or the kiss they'd shared.

He crept up behind her and wrapped his arms around his wife's curvy body. He was rock hard with anticipation, his mind racing ahead to the idea of taking her, hard, from behind, like Rod would do. She thrust back against him, just for a quick moment, and then she suddenly bristled.

"Mal, get off me!" she hissed.

Her angry tone instantly killed his boner.

"What?" he asked.

She rolled her eyes. "God, Mal, what were you thinking. Why didn't you tell me sooner? What the hell did you expect to happen tonight? What are we going to tell George?"

He backed away at the torrent of questions. "Whoa, whoa, whoa. We're not going to tell George anything," he replied, answering the last, and seemingly easiest, question.

"Oh, so we're just going to go out to dinner with them and what, just sit there and pretend that we don't know she's screwing around on him?"

"Well, yeah, it's not our place—"

"So, if Tammy and George knew I was cheating on you, you wouldn't want to know?" she demanded. "You'd just want them to sit there, pretending all was fine even though they knew I was getting fucked by another man?"

She was shaking with anger, her large breasts jiggling in her sheer bra. The sight of her, along with her words, conjured up an indelible image in his mind of his wife with another man, her boobs set in motion not by her own rage but by the rhythmic pounding of his cock. His erection returned. He shifted awkwardly to make it less obvious.

"Maybe he knows and he doesn't mind," Mal offered, though he wasn't sure he was really thinking of George at the moment.

"Tammy said he didn't."

"Tammy was stoned out of her gourd. And anyway, that's not something she might have wanted to share."

Meg gaped at him incredulously.

He continued, "Look, my point is, we don't know what's going on in that marriage. We can't just bigfoot into their relationship."

Meg seemed to grant that point, but she now shook her head sadly. "I wish you'd never told me."

"Oh, come on babe, you can't tell me I should have told you sooner and also tell me I shouldn't have told you at all."

"Don't tell me what to do," she snapped.

"Whoa, look, I don't know why you're so upset."

"No, Mal? Really? You don't? You don't see why using the revelation that one of our friends is cheating on another as, what, some sort of kinky game might backfire? What were you expecting? Me to be like, oh great, this is so *fucking* fun. Let's all become swingers. What?"

"I don't know."

"No, I think you really don't."

"Meg…."

"Mal, I think you should sleep in the guest room tonight."

"What?"

She had a look on her face he'd never seen before, manic. He felt a deep urge to tell her to relax, breathe, but he knew she'd really lose it then.

"Okay."

He turned to leave the room. As he did, she softened. "Look, we'll talk about it tomorrow."

He waited for her to invite him back, but when she didn't he slowly shuffled out of the bedroom.

"Goodnight Mal," she said softly as he closed the door behind him.

She stripped off her bra and balled up her panties, burying them in the hamper, as if to hide the evidence of her excitement. The lacy fabric was damp with her desire.

She was so angry, and yet she'd been so close to letting go. When she felt Mal's arms around her, his hard prick digging into her ass, she'd closed her eyes, imagining it was David, about to bend her over, take her hard from behind.

She couldn't do that to Mal. Couldn't let him be nothing more than a surrogate for her fantasy. She *was* mad at him and his asinine scheme. God, what had he been thinking? Didn't he know how hard she was struggling to remain faithful? No, he didn't. He couldn't. He couldn't know how tempting it was to have Tammy's example rubbed in her face. And he wouldn't. She had to keep this under wraps. The only problem is, she didn't know if she could.

Six

Mal heard the front door shut a little after six, and a moment later, the car start up and drive away. He reached for his phone. She'd sent him a text.

[Megan]: Need to go to the office for a bit.

He felt like crap. He hated to see his wife upset, and he felt responsible, even if he didn't quite understand her reaction. He'd also had a miserable, sleepless night, too worked up to do more than doze, a round-robin of images flooding his brain: Elena naked, squatting before him, sucking on his cock, her shaved snatch glistening with excitement; Tammy on her hands and knees, body squirming as Rod pounded his fat cock into her ass; but most of all Meg. Meg bent over, as he was fucking her from behind, her big tits jiggling wildly; Meg and Tammy locked in a 69, writhing against each other; and again and again, Meg with Rod. Rod with his arrogant smirk and bulging muscles.

All those images merged and melded together, and finally Mal tapped into it. God, she'd seen right through him. Seen through him before he even knew what he himself wanted. But she was right. The ultimate fantasy was for Meg to get carried away in the moment when she saw Tammy and Rod. The four of them swaying and grinding together on the dance floor. And then going away together, maybe to Rod's place.

Meg in his lap, firmly impaled on his hard cock, the two of them watching Rod and Tammy go at it. And then Rod pulling out, his fat cock stiff, beckoning Meg over to him. Feeling his cock slide out of his wife's hot, wet pussy, knowing that the next prick inside her would belong to another man. Tammy moving over to Mal, sucking his slimy cock into her mouth as Rod plunged his own tool into his wife.

It was the idea of playing with another couple that made seeing Rod and Tammy together so sexy. That was the problem with Elena. She was hot. Dirty. But he couldn't imagine sharing that experience with his wife, and as much fun as it might be to fuck a nubile, hard-bodied young woman, it would be that much better if Meg was involved in the fun.

*

Meg spent most of the morning staring out the window of her office. There *was* a big stack of work on her desk, but she couldn't even think about it quite yet. For now, she wanted a quiet place where she could think.

She was startled when her phone buzzed with an incoming text. She figured it was probably Mal, but was pleased to see it was Tammy finally responding to her own early morning message asking to talk. They agreed to meet at Mulligan's at noon.

If Meg was expecting her friend to be sheepish and embarrassed, she was quickly disabused of that notion. They talked over white wine and salads.

"Hey, duckie, what got into you last night?" Tammy asked happily, though the bags under her eyes hinted at a long night.

"Well, I know what got into you."

"Jealous?"

"Uh, no."

"You should be," Tammy smirked.

Meg shook her head. "So, are you and George splitting up?"

Tammy shrugged. "Things have never been better between us."

"So he knows?"

"I didn't say that."

Meg sighed. "Jesus, Tammy. What's going on with you. Running with another man. *Drugs.*"

"Oh, come on, it was just a little E. And we're not running around. We're just having a little fun. I'm married, not dead, you know."

"Some marriage. This would kill George if he knew."

"Would it? It would kill him to know I'm really, really happy for the first time in years. And what's the big deal. Rod is a dumb jock and a confirmed poonhound. I'm not interested in anything other than his body and he feels the same way about me."

"And you're okay with that?"

"I'm glorious with that. Meg…he does things to me…."

"I'm sure George would do those things if you told him."

Tammy rolled her eyes. "Really Meg? He's going to spank my ass and call me a whore? The first time we did it, Rod pushed me into the handicapped bathroom. He called me a cock tease. When I tried to push him away, he grabbed my wrists and held them above my head, jammed his hand under my jogging bra, pinched my nips until I whined. Then he spun me around and shoved me face first against the wall. He yanked down my pants and just pounded me into the tiles, calling me every dirty name in the book."

"Sounds like rape."

Tammy laughed. "Oh believe me, it wasn't rape. But it wasn't anything George would or could do to me. And anyway, it doesn't need to be like that. That's what I'm trying to tell you. You're hot, Meg. Like seriously hot. You can find a guy out there who'll do *whatever* you want. Shit Mal won't do, or that you wouldn't want him to do. Suck on your toes for two hours while you call him a fag. Let you fuck him up the ass with a strap-on. Whatever."

Meg blushed. "You have a heck of an imagination."

"It's called the Internet. Look it up."

"I don't know, Tam. I get what you're saying. But, it just doesn't seem like a marriage to do stuff like that."

Tammy shrugged. "Whatever floats your boat. Or doesn't."

Meg shook her head. This was all so weird. And yet, she couldn't help but think of David and his boyish charm and good looks and that shock of thick, dark hair, peering up at her from between her legs, until she begged him to fuck her with that big, thick cock of his.

Meg's lunch with Tammy left her as confused as ever. But there was one thing she knew she had to do. No, not fuck David, as deliciously tempting as that was. No, she needed to speak to Mal.

*

Mal rushed to greet her when she got home. His face was a mask of anxiety and concern.

"I'm sorry," she said quickly. "For last night."

"No, babe, I'm sorry. I was—"

"It's okay. I had lunch with Tammy."

He raised an eyebrow and tried to suppress an image of his wife and her friend, naked, making out, as he and Rod circled them like predators. He wasn't really successful. Luckily Meg misread his expression, at least partially.

"No," she laughed. "We didn't make out."

"Can't blame a guy for hoping."

"Look, Mal, we need to talk."

"Yeah, of course—"

"MO-OM!"

"Later. Tonight." She kissed him on the cheek and ran her hand playfully over his shaved head. "Now, get in character."

Mal smiled. An inside joke. The idea that they were just playing at being parents. That one day the kids would figure out that they'd been making it up as they went along.

*

The day went by slowly. Both Meg and Mal periodically retreating into their own thoughts, rousing themselves to be attentive parents. But they were also attentive to each other. Small cuddles, smiles, little reassurances to remind each other that whatever had happened, whatever *would* happen, they were in it together.

Mal finishing giving Justin lights-out and went to the master bedroom, closing, and locking, the door behind him. Meg was sitting on the bed, cross-legged in her favorite sleeping shirt, an oversized tee with a cartoon dinosaur on the front. She patted the bed and Mal sat down across from her.

"Mal, do you ever think about being with other women?"

He blanched. *Uh oh.* "No, of course not," he lied.

Mal was a terrible liar. Bad karma and all. The distress showed immediately in his face. But in this case, Meg was happy about the lie. It meant he did think of other women, and if he did, she could admit her own thoughts.

"It's okay. I…um…sometimes think of other men."

"That's only natural—"

"It's more than that. That's the reason I was so freaked out last night."

"You want to be like Tammy?"

"I didn't say that. I just want to talk about it, you know?"

Mal nodded. But no, he didn't know, couldn't quite tell where Meg was going. She was smiling, measured, maybe a little nervous, but the conversation still felt fraught.

"Talking is good."

Meg laughed.

"Mal, I just want to talk, okay? I know I was crazy last night, so I understand why you're scared of me."

"I am *not* scared of you," he replied. Still, he breathed a sigh of relief.

She took a deep breath. Even though she'd been thinking about the conversation all day, it was hard to get into it. It would be so easy for it to go badly, lead to misunderstandings.

"I don't want us to be like Tammy and George."

Mal smiled, even as he felt a rush of disappointment.

She continued. "I mean the secrets, the hiding. I don't want that to be us. I guess they never talked and now…well, here they are."

"Tammy looks like she's enjoying it."

Meg nodded. "Yeah, she is. She says Rod does things to her that George can't."

It was an expected sentiment, and yet Mal felt a rush of competing emotions. Excitement, jealousy, fear. Were there needs of Meg that he wasn't meeting? That only another man could?

"He is big."

Meg laughed. "It's not that," she replied, though in her own mind she thought, *not as big as David.* "It's more the way he acts with her. George dotes on her. Rod…." *Uses her like a slut.*

"Is a jerk," Mal completed her thought more diplomatically. Mal could feel his heart beating faster. He too doted on his wife. Did Meg long for a man like Rod, who'd dominate her? Call her names?

"Do you fantasize about him?" he asked.

"Who?"

"Rod."

"God no. I'm already married to a vapid meathead with a hot bod." She grinned.

"But you said—"

"There's a guy in my office."

Mal felt light headed. *Oh shit.* He realized he'd been blinded by his own fantasies. Had never really considered that she might have some of her own. Now suddenly, it occurred to him that it wasn't about Elena or Tammy or Rod—at least not for his wife.

Meg sensed his turmoil and tried to reassure him.

"Nothing has happened. At all. It's all in my head. Just fantasy, no flirtation."

Mal wasn't sure that was better…or worse. Uncharted waters.

"A partner?"

For some reason, Mal pictured an older man, powerful in the firm, distinguished. Salt and pepper hair, expensive suits. Mal's own insecurities played out. Meg made more than he did. Hell, his salary was almost a rounding error in their finances. And the senior partners made five times what Meg did, or more. Mal was educated, but his masters in fitness didn't quite compare to a degree from Yale law, or wherever the fuck Meg's fantasy man had gotten his degree. He almost missed her response.

"No, a junior associate."

"Yeah?" Mal replied, surprised.

"I have no idea if he even knows I exist," she added hastily.

"Other than as someone who occasionally throws work and dead-lines at him."

Meg's guilt flared. She knew that wasn't quite true. Why had she said it? She'd wanted to come clean. *That* was the plan. Fishing for compliments?

Mal bit. "Babe, there is not a man around who doesn't know you exist."

She blushed. Even after all these years, it still gave her a thrill to know that Mal, hardbodied, fitness freak Mal, found her attractive.

"I mean, I don't know that he's interested."

"Well, you're his boss. You could always order him, right?"

Meg laughed it off, but *fuck*, that was a hot thought. Again, she imagined David between her legs. *Don't stop.*

Mal saw his wife's cheeks flush. It wasn't what he'd been fan-tasizing, but the idea of his wife dominating a young boy toy struck him as weirdly exciting…and somehow, safe.

"I wouldn't mind," he said quickly.

Meg paused. She'd always been more analytical, and now, re-alizing they were close to a life-changing discussion, she hesitated, seeking clarity.

"Mind what?"

"If you…I don't know. Jeez, Meg. I…I trust you. And…I want you be happy. And…I don't know…if you want to go for it…with him…I…could…"

He trailed off, out of words.

Meg shook her head. "I don't need this." Another half-truth. "But, if you're in the same place. You know, if you're also thinking about…other people…then…I don't know. *Are you?*"

There was a weird urgency in her tone. Responding to that as much as anything else, he replied, "Yes."

"Tell me."

"There's this…um…girl. She comes to my classes. I think, I guess…she flirts with me."

"Is she cute?"

Mal nodded vigorously even as he gave a measured response. "I guess. I mean, yeah, she's young, fit."

Of course. That was always Meg's concern. All those young, tight, slutty little girls swooning over Mal's zero body fat, his hippy-dippy new-agey talk of energy flows and balance and, what, fucking crystals or something. And yet, that was the one problem she'd dealt with long ago. They'd been together over a decade. She knew she couldn't compete on body fat, but Mal had chosen her, big boobs, soft ass, and all, and she wasn't worried that some little whore with a six-pack would take him away.

"What's her name?"

"Elena," he replied. "And your boy toy?"

She flushed, felt a surge of excitement at the use of the term.

"David."

"So what are we talking about?" he asked.

Meg paused. The moment of truth. *Shit.* It felt like the moment they'd jumped out of that fucking airplane. Go or no go. She'd vowed *never* to do that again. But now, peering out over the sheer drop, she couldn't resist.

"I don't want an open marriage…"

Mal resisted the urge to complete the thought. He needed to let Meg do it.

"…and I don't want this to be a habit…."

Oh God, she was really….

"…and I don't want any lies…."

Mal's breath caught.

"…but if you're interested…."

He was, he was so interested.

"…then maybe, we could, try, um, an experiment."

Mal hesitated, then proceeded. "An experiment named David?"

"And Elena," she replied. "I'm not doing this unless you're interested in experimenting,' too."

"And what are the rules?"

"No lies," Meg replied, feeling immediately guilty. She'd already skirted the truth several times.

"No lies," Mal acknowledged, though he too realized he hadn't completely come clean either.

*

Mal excused himself to the bathroom. He needed to get ready for bed, but he also needed to stop his head from spinning. He was a go-with-the-flow kind of guy, but this was intense even for him.

Had they really just agreed to sleep with other people? And what did "experiment" really mean? What if the experiment went well?

Mal was hard. There was no hiding it, so he didn't bother. He brushed his teeth. He stripped out of his shirt and jeans, and headed back into the bedroom in just his boxer-briefs and his obvious erection.

Meg had stripped out of her oversized t-shirt. She was naked. And she was gorgeous. Her long red hair tumbled around her pale shoulders, thick, unruly, and inherently sexy. She was leaning back on her arms, her full breasts bare, capped with high, coral-hued nipples. Her legs were crossed, one foot up on the bed, the other dangling off, lazy and relaxed. Even from the door and in the low light, Mal could see her dampness glisten on her thick mat of curls.

For her part, the sight of her husband in just his boxer-briefs practically took her breath away. Was she really okay with unleashing him on some hard-bodied slut? Or was she doing that just to justify getting together with David?

"Hey," he said.

"Hey yourself."

He crossed the room, muscles moving beneath his dark skin like some exotic predictor. She tightened her thighs as he crawled onto the bed, pressing his knee between them. He kissed her, long and deep, and for a moment, she thought of him kissing another woman.

Jealousy surged through her, nearly blinding everything. Nearly. Beneath it all was a spark of something strange, something unexpected—excitement.

She trailed her hands down his back, digging her thumbs into his tight underwear. With a tug, she pulled them down, freeing his cock. He had a nice cock, above average and well suited to his body. She'd never had anything to complain about, but still...David had her curious. She'd had an ex who was bigger than average, but David seemed to be in a whole other class. What would that be like?

"You're so wet," Mal said as he sank into you. "That can't just be me without a shirt."

Meg laughed. "Did I ever tell you that you're so full of it?"

"Maybe once or twice." He found a steady, easy rhythm with her. "So are you thinking of this guy? David?"

Her heart fluttered as her husband used David's name. "That's definitely part of it."

Mal's cock surged. *David. Someone new. Someone unexpected.* He was still trying to wrap his head around it.

"And do I have Elena to thank for this?" She squeezed his cock with her pussy.

Elena. How could Mal forget about Elena? In his anxiety—or whatever—of thinking about Meg with another man, he'd nearly forgotten about his side of the deal. He thought about Elena yesterday, about how good she looked in those tiny shorts and sports bra. He'd just been given a free pass to play, guilt free. *Yes, please.*

"You're thinking about her, aren't you?" Meg said.

Mal didn't know whether to feel guilty or not, and for a moment, he wasn't sure how to answer her. Then he remembered their agreement. *No lies.* "Yes."

"Good, because I'm so thinking about David."

"Like what?" Mal asked before he could help himself.

Like watching his expression the first time I suck his cock, she thought, but didn't say. "Like how I'm going to seduce him."

"Time to go shopping for more sexy, little power suits." Mal was joking, but he was on to something. Her suits were getting a little stale. "Maybe pull out the garter belt and stockings—"

"Hey, mister. This is my fantasy, not yours."

Mal shrugged. "Just saying. All men like the look."

"And what about you? What's your plan of attack?"

"Me? Plan?" They laughed together. "I was planning on just grabbing her after class and doing her on her yoga mat."

The crazy thing, he realized, was that he could probably do exactly that. Elena would probably be down for something like that. He'd lock the door after the last customer left. She'd know. She'd come on to him. Kiss him. They'd tear off what little clothes that they had. She'd lay back in her chair, spread her legs, crook her finger at him—

"Oh, fuck me...David!" Meg's voice shattered the fantasy. "How did you know I like it hard?"

"Because I know exactly what a slut like you needs." Mal wasn't sure if he was talking to Elena here, or Meg, but as the words tumbled out, they rang true either way.

"Yes. Fuck me. Fuck me with your big, hard cock."

"Let's see how flexible you are," Mal said. He raised Meg's legs over his shoulders, folding her in half. "Pretty damn flexible."

"God, you're hitting me so deep!" Meg groaned. That wasn't a lie. At this angle, Mal hit her in places that he usually didn't. Was this a preview of what David had in store? Would he make her scream? "I'm close. I'm close. Do me harder!"

Mal closed his eyes, first seeing Elena moaning beneath him, begging to be fucked. He rammed harder, their hips slapping loudly with each thrust. Her tits bounced between them. Her face contorted.

"You close, baby?" Meg asked, her voice breaking with strain.

"I'm close."

"Come, baby. Give me your come!"

Elena disappeared, replaced by his wife. His Meg. With some faceless stranger—some young buck—who was giving it to her hard. Who was about to explode inside of her.

"Take it," he growled. "Feel it!"

He exploded deep inside her, pushing her over the edge. Fantasy, reality, possibility, anxiety—it all tangling together as their orgasms washed into one another. When they came down from that high, sweat cooling on their naked bodies, they were together again, husband and wife, ready to take this next, scary step.

Seven

They'd made love again on Sunday. Twice! That was definitely a first since the kids were born. Okay, so it was once in the morning, and once in the evening, but even still.

The morning sex was a treat. There were already sounds of little feet in the house. Demands for parental attention were surely imminent, which gave their coupling a quiet urgency. They'd been spooning naked, Meg enjoying the feel of her husband's hard body, his partial erection. She just had to grind her ass against him a few times to get his attention. He was easy that way, as Elena was surely about to discover. No. Not this time. This was about her and Mal.

She reached back and stroked his cock then pressed the head against her lips. She was aroused, but not soaked. She enjoyed it like that sometimes. She knew Mal would take it slow, and she liked the sensation of his cock opening her up, the friction of it, like she was some little virgin taking her first prick rather than a mother of three. She wondered if it would be like that every time with David and his huge cock…. No, she banished that thought as well. She wanted to stay in the moment. *Mindfulness* as Mal would say.

Mal entered her slowly, as she knew he would. He reached around and caressed her stomach. She sucked in her gut instinctively, though she knew she was slim enough, and anyway, Mal seemed to liked the way she was a little rounded everywhere, though surely Elena was rock hard…. *No!* He massaged upward, lodging his hands between her breasts. She smiled. He loved her cleavage. Eyes, hands, kisses, he always lingered there. He'd never seemed interested in pressing his cock between her mounds. He seemed to regard it as almost a holy place, not to be defiled. David on the other hand…. *Stop!* Be mindful.

She felt him nuzzle in close, his hot breath on her neck, his lips finding that little spot of sensitive skin beneath her ear that always drove her wild. He kissed her softly there, just brushing his lips against her. She moaned softly. He began to move faster. Her breaths quickened. They came simultaneously, not explosively, but tenderly.

She giggled. "That was pro."

"Practice makes perfect."

It was true. Whatever the appeal of novelty, there was something to be said for ordinary, married sex. *Mindfulness.*

"DA-AD!" yelled Angela.

"MO-OM!" bellowed Justin.

They both laughed. That could only mean one thing. The kids were fighting and trying to make their parents take sides. Fat chance, kiddies.

*

Mal wasn't quite sure how to proceed. He sat at the trainer's desk scanning the club. He was there to answer questions and keep an eye out for mishaps on the floor. He owed an hour of desk time for every three hours of classes he taught, but now, Monday morning, after 9:00am it was dead and he had time to think.

They'd agreed to experiment. Cool. Did that mean, like, right now? He wasn't sure. It was all very strange. They'd agreed on a single rule, "no lies." And then they'd shared some fantasies, but he was suddenly wondering about the logistics of it.

"No lies" implied at the very least coming clean if—*when*—anything happened. But did it require prior warning? Were dates allowed? Or just encounters? Overnights?

"Hey, man, damn, you're wife is hot." Rod had sauntered up.

"Uh, thanks."

"I would totally wreck that."

Mal leaned back in his chair. Mal prided himself on being cool, calm, collected. Mellow. Still, he eyed Rod, sizing him up. Rod was bigger, stronger, but slower, clumsier. In a confined space Rod would have the upper hand. Out in the open, Mal thought could take him.

"That's my wife you're talking about."

Rod shrugged, backing down. "Just sayin'."

Mal didn't say anything.

"Tammy says we should get together," he added.

Funny. That had been Mal's fantasy as well. But now he was having second thoughts. He didn't like the idea of Rod and Tammy plotting about him and his wife.

"She thinks…Meg, is it? She thinks Meg might be into it."

Mal chortled. He stood. "Rod, buddy, believe me, if my wife is ever the least bit interested in getting together with you, we'll talk about it. But for now, how about you and Tammy focus on some other couple?"

Rod smirked. "Whatever man. I'm just sayin', I could show her a good time."

Mal shook his head. "Alright, you take the desk. I got shit to do."

As he walked away, he probed his reaction. Rod had only proposed what he'd been thinking himself. So why was he upset? Why weren't they, even now, plotting ways to bring Meg, apparently the only holdout, into the scene? It didn't make sense. Yet there it was.

It occurred to Mal that this whole experiment thing might be more complicated than it first seemed.

*

It was peculiar. She had a free pass now. In theory she could have pulled David into her office and fucked him that very morning. All of a sudden, she didn't want to. The fever had broken. She chuckled to herself. Funny how that works.

But slowly the fantasy returned. Part of it was her calendar. It showed two weeks at a time, and sure enough, there, right in the middle of next week were three, full-day, dark blue blocks. California. *With David.*

She'd mentioned the trip to Mal when it was first scheduled, three weeks out, but with the usual caveats: this is tentative, the case might settle, just keep your schedule open just in case. And those caveats were also, she explained to herself, why she hadn't mentioned that David was scheduled to come along. Why get Mal all worked up for something that might yet fall through? But now three weeks out had turned to ten days and then seven, and the travel was looking more and more likely.

Those dark blue blocks, though, weren't just making her think about Mal, but about David. Or more precisely, Mal's question about David. So far, her fantasies had just been about the act, about David's big cock and the various things she'd do to him and he'd do her. But now, her mind turned to the seduction.

Would she tempt him into making the first move? An extra button undone on her blouse. Hiking up her skirt to adjust her thigh highs when she "didn't think he was looking." Lingering gazes. "Accidentally" brushing up against him. She wondered how long he'd resist the temptation. She was his boss after all, but he was also a man.

Or would she be more bold? Invite him to her room for a drink. Greet him at the door in a loosely tied hotel bathrobe. Sit across from him, crossing and uncrossing her legs so he could spy her naked pussy.

Or, perhaps, most out of character and maybe most exciting, would she simply take charge? Invite him to her office and tell him outright that she wanted more from him than legal support. *Once we get to LA, I want not just your mind, but your body. You can do that for me, can't you David?* Grab his tie, yank him to his knees, lift up her skirt, and press his face to her snatch.

Meg gasped as she touched herself...in the shower at the gym... in her office...in the car on the way to work...even lying in bed beside Mal as he soundly slept. She was trying to be mindful and focused when she was with her husband, but the rest of the time, the majority of the time, her mind was increasingly consumed with David and their forthcoming time together three thousand miles away from home.

*

It came as a shock to Mal. Damn, his wife was going to California with another man. As unsettling as the news was the way she broke it. A forced casualness that betrayed her deep excitement. She didn't admit it, but he could tell she'd been thinking about it, *a lot.*

Their love life had been on fire recently. Every night, and even being interrupted by the kids merely delaying their lovemaking rather than deferring it as had often happened in the past.

Last night, after she broke the news, as they snuggled naked in bed, he'd asked her if she was thinking of David. She denied it.

She said that whatever happened with other people, she wanted their time together to be, as much as possible, their own. Mal agreed, but his mind refused to cooperate.

When she sucked his cock, all he could think about was that she would soon be doing the same to another man. When he hefted her breasts and teased her nipples, he knew that soon it would be David enjoying his wife's amazing chest. And when he entered her, he was constantly aware that in just a few days it would be someone else inside her, enjoying her tightness and her wetness, making her moan and sigh in passion.

The disconcerting feeling persisted even after they kissed and separated, retreating to their own sides of the bed to sleep. And it even persisted as he finished up his class the next morning.

"Hey, Mal, that was a great class."

It was Elena, her mat rolled up and slung over her shoulder, rocking back and forth excitedly before him. She looked extra cute today, hair in a ponytail, a sheen of sweat on her forehead.

He smiled at her. "You're doing great. Your Scorpion was super."

She beamed. "Thanks, but I really want to move on from fore-arm stands to hand stands."

"You're getting there."

"Maybe I could have a private lesson," she suggested.

"Yeah, definitely. Email me and we'll set something up."

She nodded. "Cool…. Oh, hey, I don't know if you're into this sort of thing. But, there's this cool happy hour, at Lucky Wongs, to-morrow evening. Friday? Well, you know it's Friday. I mean, there'll be a bunch of folks there…and…it's usually fun…. I don't know if you're into that."

She was babbling and he could see the excitement in her face, that mixture of anticipation and anxiety when you actually make a move on someone you're crushing on. He had a free pass. An experiment. And yet, he knew he'd have normally begged off. Dragged it out. But with Meg's revelation, it suddenly seemed like the right thing to do. If she was going to go to California with David, he surely could have a drink or two with Elena. Still….

"That sounds really fun. I'll try to make it. I just need to make sure my kids are with someone." That's the problem with dating while married. Who's going to watch the kids when you're out sucking face with a stranger?

He could see her trying to read his face. Had they just made a date, or had he just brushed her off?

He gave her a reassuring smiled. She patted him on the arm. "Okay, I hope to see you."

She turned and walked out of the studio. *Damn*, she had a fine ass.

Eight

"Are you sure you're okay with this?" Mal asked for the fifth time.

"I'm sure. Go. Have *fun*."

Mal searched her face for any signs of a test. He'd mentioned the happy hour invitation, but had put all kinds of qualifications around it—all kinds of opportunities for her to tell him to stay. She didn't. Not even once. Now, he was going.

"I'll see you later," he said, kissing her softly on the mouth. That didn't seem right considering the circumstances, so he grabbed her again and pulled her in for a long, hard kiss.

"Text me with...updates," she said.

He nodded. "Okay."

And then he was out the door. He was free. It felt weird to be so untethered. He lived most of his life that way, but this was different. This was more than just a philosophical state. This wasn't a mindset. This was fucking real. If he wanted to, he could be pounding Elena's hard ass within the hour.

By the time he arrived, happy hour was nearly over. In fact, technically, it *was* over, it being just after 7. Elena's group was still going strong, though, crowded around the bar with rail drinks in their hands.

Mal felt old. Her friends were all in her twenties, like her. He would be forty in a few months. Suddenly, he regretted coming.

"Mal, you made it!" Elena shouted before he could get away. She looked amazing as always, although he realized that this was the first time he'd seen her anything other than exercise clothes.

"Hey, Elena," Mal said, turning on his charm. "Sorry I'm late. Was hard to get away, you know."

He realized that there was very little chance that anyone in this group had kids, let alone was married.

"Everyone, this is Malik. Mal, this is everyone."

"Hey, everyone," he said.

Elena gave him a huge hug, and for a second, he wondered if she was going to go ahead and kiss him, too. He could smell the vodka on her breath when she looked up at him and said, "I'm so glad you made it."

"You're right, Elly, he's totally hot," one of Elena's friends said.

Elena looked at her—a slender woman with a sharp blonde bob and dazzling blue eyes—but didn't step away from Mal. "Back away, Zoe, I saw him first."

"I just said he was hot's all." Zoe laughed, adding, "Whore."

Elena looked at Mal, genuine embarrassment in her face. "It's how we talk to each other when we've been drinking."

Zoe scoffed before Elena shushed her.

At last, Elena stepped back and gave him a once over. "You clean up well, teach."

He hadn't dressed up—Mal almost never dressed up—but he'd thrown a nicer shirt than normal on over his jeans, and even donned socks with his shoes.

Elena, on the other hand, looked like a fucking model. Her dress—a sundress, he supposed—was sexy as hell. Yellow, haltered, and short enough to show off plenty of leg when she moved. He'd seen her in much less over the last few weeks, but there was something sexy about seeing her all dolled up.

"I like your...hair," he said, pulling his eyes from the cleavage created by the halter.

Elena touched the dark braids she'd done in her hair—a dirty Heidi look—and smiled. "Glad you noticed."

"The man needs a drink," someone said

"What'll it be? We've got an open tab."

Mal looked at the taps. "I'll take a PBR."

"Coming right up."

*

Meg felt numb. She'd watched her husband climb into his car to go off and meet some other girl. A huge part of her screamed at how wrong this was. How stupid. She'd been Elena once. She'd been the one to attract Mal's eye in class, to flirt with him, to win his heart. Was she opening things up for disaster?

When panic began to take hold, she fought it down with cold, hard logic. Mal had three kids that he loved. He loved her, too. No matter what this girl, Elena, did for him, she could never replace all that history.

The end result? She was numb. She didn't want to think about what was happening out at happy hour, so she didn't.

Her phone buzzed as she headed upstairs to start the bedtime routines. Her heart fluttered. Either it was Mal with a quick check in, or it was—

[David]: you started to pack yet?

David. She sighed like a fucking schoolgirl. This was a new

thing. She decided to give him her number since they were going to be spending time together out in LA and email wasn't always convenient. She was surprised when the first text came in, but then she figured it made sense, more or less. His generation didn't *call* anyone. Phones were for texts, not talking. And besides, the texts had all been about work, all innocent enough.

[Megan]: Not yet. You?

[David]: was just about to start. ties?

For one weak moment, Megan imagined herself tied to his hotel bed, silk neckties about her wrists, her legs splayed—

[Megan]: Yes, bring ties. A mediator is just like a judge, even in LA.

[David]: Yes, ma'am.

[Megan]: Don't ma'am me, junior.

[David]: lol

"Mom, where are my PJs?!" Justin yelled.

Meg sighed and put her phone away. Later. Later.

*

"So what do you actually do?" Mal asked Elena. They were alone in the crowd, the group having dispersed as the others went off to meet up with other friends. Zoe was the last to leave, but when she did leave she whispered to Elena, *I get him next.*

"I'm a law student," Elena said.

"Really?" He didn't say, *My wife's a lawyer,* although he almost did. Bringing up Meg would not have been appropriate, considering the inappropriateness of the night.

"Why is that surprising?"

"I...."

Elena laughed. "Don't worry, you're not the first guy to think I am just a pretty face."

"It's not that." But really, it was. "You just seem more carefree than I usually...think of lawyers."

"Ah. Well, I'll grant you that. It's why none of my friends we just hung out with were from law school. And probably why I spend so much time in your studio."

Mal feigned a frown. "And here I was, thinking you were coming to see me."

Elena stepped close to him, touching his chest. "Well, there's that, too."

Mal tensed. Elena was close enough that he could smell the fresh scent of her shampoo. He could feel the heat of her body. If there was a time to kiss her, now was it. But....

He thought of Tammy and Rodney, so brazen in their infidelity. Lucky Wongs was even less discreet than *Pumped*. Chances of him knowing someone in the crowd were high.

Elena seemed to read his mind. "Want to get out of here? My place isn't too far away."

Mal's chest tightened, right along with his pants. Could he do this?

"I should be getting back soon. I'm expected."

Elena didn't pout, or even look very disappointed. She also didn't hesitate to say, "Then just walk me back. I'd feel safer with a big, strong man beside me."

"Sure. Let's just settle up the bill."

*

Meg started to plan her outfits for her trip. David's texts had her considering what to bring, and anyway, it was easier to focus on packing than dwelling on whatever Mal was doing. She hadn't received a text from him since he'd left nearly two hours ago, so her mind was all over the place.

She laid out four suits—one for each day on the ground, plus an extra just in case. She made sure to pack the pinstriped dress suit because she knew how flattering that was on her—and how professional it could be with its matching jacket. The other two were what Mal called her little power suits, pencil skirts with tailored jackets. Theoretically, she could wear either without a blouse if she buttoned the jackets all the way, but she'd never done that. Maybe next week...

The final was a suit she'd just purchased and never worn. She didn't think that she could ever wear it. She'd bought it on impulse. Not that it was overly scandalous, but it was by far the shortest of any she owned, the snug skirt ending well above her knees. It was a skirt to project a confident, powerful exec. A skirt designed to show off her legs, and to do so brazenly. She could just imagine the attention she'd get in it....

...which is why she'd never wear it. Still, she brought it anyway.

Her lingerie was a different matter. The racy things she chose were things that she *could* wear. She'd taken Mal's advice and packed her one and only garter belt, the matching bra and panties, and had gone out and purchased some stockings and thigh-highs. If she was going to be showing off her legs, then she wasn't going to be doing so in pantyhose. She threw in her black, satin negligée for sleeping—if she was going to sleep in anything at all, she thought with a blush—leaving the oversized sleep shirt in her wardrobe.

The final item of clothing she packed was a party dress. They were headed out to LA. She knew the score. There was a high likelihood that they'd go out one of the nights, and she didn't want to resort to wearing a suit to a trendy cocktail lounge. She may be 35, but she didn't want David to think of her as old, or, heaven forbid, "mature."

The dress wasn't new, although it may have been close to eight years since she'd put it on. She didn't even know if it fit. Only one way to find out.

The dress was black, of course, because if you were only going to own one small dress, black was most sensible. It was short, of course, to make sure that it qualified as "little." And it was tight, which turned out to be its saving grace. While she kept herself in shape with frequent visits to the gym—especially in the last few weeks— she wasn't in her twenties anymore. Her hips were wider. Her breasts were fuller. No amount of time on the eliptical would change that.

Luckily, the LBD accommodated her curvier body. If anything, it looked even better on her now than it had when she'd been skinnier. There was nothing fancy about it. The straps at her shoulders were wide enough to allow her to wear a bra—a necessary evil for her—but the front still plunged low enough to present a tempting view between her breasts. She giggled. David wouldn't have a chance.

Padding barefoot to her closet, she removed her tallest pair of shoes: black pumps with stiletto heels and red leather soles. She'd need to get a pedicure before heading out to LA, she thought, wiggling the tips of her toes through the opening at the base of her heels. Turning, she regarded herself objectively and had to admit, she looked good. The dress did wonders to the extra padding in her ass, and the four-inch heels did even better things to her legs.

She imagined David, standing before her, admiring her in this dress. She thought of his easy, boyish smile as his eyes traveled along her body. She'd crook a finger at him and he'd come like a trained dog. She'd point at the ground, and he'd sink to her knees before her. She shivered. This fantasy of being worshipped was a new one to her, but it was strong.

Meg went back to her lingerie drawer and pulled out one more thing—her glass dildo. That would get packed, too, just in case things didn't play out the way she hoped they would. It was constructed of clear glass with a swirling pattern of pink and blue locked inside. It was mostly shaped like a hard shaft, although the tip featured several knobs that felt so damn good on her g-spot. She'd never been a fan of the more realistic dildos, but for the first time, part of her wished she had one. It would have made the fantasy so much better.

She sat back on the edge of the bed, careful not to rumple the clothes she'd laid out, and hiked up the dress. She hadn't bothered with panties, and her pubic hair was already matted with excitement. Her bush. She'd have to do something about that, too. David was young, and Meg was well aware of the current trends. Besides, it wouldn't do to have him think that she wasn't a natural redhead, even though she was.

But first….

"Ah…." she groaned, pushing the glass into her pussy. It was about as thick as Mal at the tip, but quickly got wider, the deeper she pushed it in. Thinking of David, she pushed it in almost as deep as she could take, feeling herself open up around it.

Maybe she'd make David use this on her first. Worship her, show her how much he wanted her. She dipped the dildo in and out of her, making sure those knobs hit all her special spots. With her free hand, she rubbed her clit, imagining instead that she was raking it through David's thick, dark hair—so very different from Mal's shaved head.

Would he be tamed so easily, she wondered. Did she want him to? The fantasy shifted as her orgasm neared. David stood, his lean body naked, his huge cock not even fully erect as it hung between his legs. *Your turn*, he'd say, the worship gone from his voice. She imagined the way he'd reach forward and guide her head onto his cock. She drove the dildo in harder, thinking about taking him into her mouth, of feeling him swell and harden as she blew him. She bit her lip, angling the knobs so they struck her g-spot over and over. She shut her eyes tighter, her mouth watering at the thought of David's cockhead passing into the back of her throat. Would he be surprised that she could deep-throat a cock? Would he expect it?

The fantasy shifted once again. The dildo became his cock, slamming into her. Fucking all sense out of her. She stifled a scream, but out there, thousands of miles from home, she'd let loose. She'd scream for David. For his cock. For his come. She could almost hear their skin slapping. Could feel his balls swing against her ass as he prepared to explode inside of her.

Come. Come, David. I want to feel it. I want to feel your heat!

She rocked back, stretching out on the mattress as she rammed the dildo deeper and deeper. Knees up, legs spread, only her ass and her shoulders touching the bed, she came with the force of a bullet leaving its chamber.

*

"You've got a nice place here," Mal said, looking around. Looking everywhere, in fact, other than at his host. "Roommates?"

"Just little old me," Elena said, going to the kitchen to pour them each a glass of water. How had he let himself get talked into coming up? He'd fully intended on leaving her outside the front of her building, but she'd convinced him to come up for a glass of water before going home.

Instead of thinking about where things were clearly headed, though, he focused on her digs. He wondered how a law student could afford a one bedroom downtown.

Again, Elena seemed to read his mind. "I've got a nice scholarship," she explained. "See, even smarter than you thought, huh?"

Mal finally looked in her direction. She was leaning against the island counter of her kitchen, a single, tall glass of water in her hand. He'd never thought of a woman drinking water as sensuous, but Elena did it in a way that had him wishing he were the glass.

Of course, he didn't just look at her lips and the glass. He looked at her, and his heart sped up at what he saw. The yellow dress was somehow both sexy and demure, neither too tight, too short, or too slutty. This wasn't a desperate girl out on the prowl. She was the kind of woman who knew what she wanted and took it.

As if to prove it, she said, "Are you going to make the first move, or are you waiting for me to do that?"

"I…" Mal's mouth went dry. He looked at the water in her hand. "I'm married"

Elena ignored him, following his eyes. "Want a sip?" she asked with a smirk. "Come here."

Mal shouldn't have gone. He really, really shouldn't have. He knew it. But he went anyway, closing the distance between them on wooden legs. Elena's dark eyes flashed. She took a sip of water, but didn't immediately swallow. Instead, she pulled him into a kiss—a wet, watery kiss. It spilled out between them, down their chins, dripping onto their clothes, but at that point, neither cared. They were too preoccupied with the slippery sensation of their tongues meeting for the first time.

Mal's first kiss with another woman in over ten years couldn't have been better. The wrongness of the sensation only added to the excitement. Elena didn't kiss like Meg. She didn't taste like Meg. She wasn't fucking Meg. She was her own woman—another woman—and he was really, really turned on by it.

Elena pulled back, wicked elation in her smile. "I seem to have gotten my dress wet," she said.

Before Mal could slow things down—before he could even make up his mind that that's what he wanted—Elena reached behind her neck and unclasped the halter. She shifted back a half-step and shrugged out of the dress. She was naked beneath. Completely naked.

Mal's breath caught as his eyes traveled down her nudity. Her body was as close to perfect as he'd ever seen. She was slender, yet toned, saving her from being too skinny. Her breasts sat high and round, a healthy handful—and fuller than he'd expected—giving way to her flat, sweeping stomach with the beginnings of a six-pack beneath. Lower still, past her narrow hips to her pussy, as bare and hairless as he'd imagined it would be. She was wet, her lips swollen, her clit already pushing free.

"There, that's better," she said.

Mal looked back up at her face, color blooming in his cheeks. Elena reached out and touched his shirt, where some of the water had dripped. "Looks like you got a little wet, too."

"Don't worry about it…" he said, his voice trailing off as she began to unbutton his shirt. This was it. This was the point of no return. Once that was off—

"Elena, I should be…. I need to get—"

"Going?" She raised an eyebrow at him. "You sure about that? I think part of you would rather be *coming*."

He jumped as he felt her hand cup his crotch, squeezing his heavy balls and swollen cock.

She leaned into him, kissing down his neck and along his exposed collarbone. "You're free to leave, of course," she whispered. Even as she said it, though, she sank to her knees, her hands deftly working the zipper of his jeans open. She looked up at him, her eyes never leaving his. "You sure that's what you really want to do?"

Mal stood frozen, helpless as she opened his pants and freed his cock. He was beyond hard. The tip of his cock peeked out over the band of his boxer-briefs, and he sprang free as she yanked them down. "It's beautiful," she whispered, shortly before closing her lips over it.

Mal groaned, clutching the counter beside him to maintain his balance. It took three strokes for Elena to find a rhythm. After that, he was lost. She was so different than Meg—faster, swifter, more aggressive. He looked down at her, searching for the will to pull back, to pull away, but couldn't. Maybe it was those eyes, dark and passionate, never shying away from eye contact. They watched him watch her, loving every moment of it.

Her hands worked in time with her mouth, caressing his balls, jacking the lower shaft. He felt wrung out after just thirty seconds of the blowjob, but knew that he wanted to last longer—needed to last longer. So he closed his eyes and tried to think of other things—non-erotic things. He thought of his lesson plans, the inversions workshop he had next week. He drew on his yoga training, calming his mind. He thought about Meg with the kids and—

None of that shit worked. Elena's blowjob twisted everything. Lesson plans turned into fucking Elena in the studio. The inversions workshop made him wonder if he could fuck her doing a handstand.

And any thought of Meg turned into thoughts of Meg in LA

next week. Of Meg in this very same position with another man, her head racing up and down that guy David's length. He wondered if David were bigger than him. Was that important to Meg? She'd never said anything about it. Would he use her? Would he debase her? Would he press his shaft between her tits and use them like Mal never had the courage to do?

"Look at me," Elena demanded.

Mal did, returning to the moment. Returning to this younger woman on her knees, naked, servicing him.

"Don't hold back, baby," she said, jerking him rapidly. "One thing you need to learn about me, it's that I don't like my lovers holding back."

Her stroking hand grew faster, squeezing harder. Almost too hard.

"You ready to come?" she asked.

Mal knew better than to lie. He nodded.

"Good. I'm ready to take it." She dipped low, swirling her tongue along the crown of his cock. "Does your wife ever take it on the face?"

Mal shook his head, which only coaxed an evil grin from Elena.

"Come on my face, Mal. I want to feel it all over my cheeks. My tits. My neck. Do it. Don't think. Do. It."

Mal lost the thread of whatever she was saying. His breath caught. His world buzzed. He exploded, sending a ropey blast of come across her cheek. Her eyes lit up as she took the second on the bridge of her nose. She directed him lower, catching the next few on her tits. Her smile only grew wider and wider.

"Yes, baby. Come all over me." She was practically moaning. That's when he realized that her left hand was down between her thighs, two fingers pressing into her cunt. She threw her head back and came herself as the last of Mal's gooey mess struck her on her long, slender neck.

Elena sighed, looking up at him. Gracefully, she scooped up the splatter of come on her nose and sucked her finger. "Thanks for coming out for happy hour."

Now that the moment had passed, horror descended over Mal. He took a step back, hitting the counter.

"Will you be at the studio Monday?" she asked.

"Y-yeah."

"Good. I'll swing by and we can arrange my private lesson."

He didn't know what to say, so he nodded. Elena helped him pull his jeans back into place before turning and going to the sink to rinse the rest of his come off her. She still wore her heels, he noted guiltily, and her ass looked fucking amazing naked like that. He thought about Rodney's promise to Tammy about taking her ass. Was that something Elena was into?

He shook his head. "I'll...see you in a couple of days."

Where was his cool now? Where was his inner calm? He felt jittery all over.

Cleaned up, Elena paced over to him, once again giving him an open view of her full-frontal nudity. She pressed close, still smelling slightly of his come, and kissed him. "See you then," she whispered, squeezing his cock.

He practically ran away.

*

Meg stood in front of the mirror of the bathroom, naked and pink from the shower. She traced her hands down her body, cupping her full tits, feeling their weight, before moving lower. Tentatively, she touched her mound, skimming her fingers across the now bare skin. It had been years since she'd shaved, and as she shuddered at the sensitivity of her bald pussy, she wondered why she'd ever stopped.

She wondered what Mal would say when he discovered what she'd done. He'd never shown a preference either way, but he was like that—sometimes too easy going. Sometimes, she wished that he'd be more forward with his needs. Even the idea of this experiment had been hers.

And yet he was the first to take advantage of their new relationship. He still hadn't texted. That was almost three hours of radio silence. Her gut squirmed. *This was a good thing*, she assured herself. It removed any guilt she might have felt when she thought about David.

Her fingers slid between her thighs, touching her freshly shaved snatch. It was so soft. So delicate. She couldn't wait to feel David's mouth on it—

The front door opened and closed. Her heart skipped. Mal was back.

Suddenly self-conscious of her nudity, she pulled on her fluffy robe and met Mal at the door to the bedroom.

"You're still awake," he said, freezing at the top of the stairs. Was that guilt on his face?

Meg squeezed her hands together. "Did you….?"

He shook his head. Part of her breathed a sigh of relief. Part of her was disappointed. Had he backed out? Gotten cold feet?

He walked up to her, his smile overcoming any look of remorse and sheepishness. He gathered her in his arms and kissed her. Something was different in the kiss, and in the way he smelled. She pulled back and looked up at him questioningly.

He stepped past her, closing the door. "I didn't sleep with her, but that doesn't mean nothing happened…."

Mal's heart was racing. Be truthful. Be honest. No lies.

Meg looked up at him, her eyes wide, inquisitive. She was beautiful. How could he do this to her?

"What happened?"

He reached down and touched her face, feeling how soft her cheek was under his thumb. "Everything happened so fast. We went back to her place…. I swear, I was just going to walk her back…and then she invited me up to her apartment for water. I didn't know…. I couldn't think of a way…."

"It's okay, Mal. Slow down." She reached up, mirroring his touch on his own face. His cheeks were scruffy and flushed. She liked that. "I'm not mad. I promise."

He nodded, drawing a steadying breath. "We kissed."

Meg felt like a wave had swelled up out of no where and tried to knock her down. She weathered it with nothing but a gasp. "What else?"

"She…" He hesitated. Meg stared, enthralled. The air felt syrupy between them. He pressed on. "She went down on me."

For one long, uncomfortable moment, nothing was said. Time stood still, frozen and delicate. Then Mal gave one of his easy smiles, crinkling the corners of his eyes, and the tension melted away.

"Did you enjoy it?"

"No lies, right?" He took a deep breath and nodded. What he left off was that he'd finished on her face, but admitting this much was hard enough!

"Naughty, naughty boy," Meg said. She drew him close again and kissed him. It was easier to deal with than she thought, now that it was out there. "Did you return the favor?"

Mal felt the same sense of relief. "Not yet," he said.

Meg's eyes flashed. "So you're going to see her again?"

"She said she'd stop by the studio Monday. She's interested in a private lesson."

Meg laughed. "Of course she is."

"Maybe I'll set something up while you're in California. After all, I'm going to need someone to keep me company when you're not here to do it."

Someone *other* than the kids who he realized would be taking up most of his time.

They kissed again, deeper this time. Meg curled her hands into fists at his side. Mal pulled his shirt over his head without fully un-buttoning it, and she ran her hand through his chest hair, down over his hard pectorals. Mal's touch went to the robe around her waist, loosening it, tugging it off.

They crossed the room like that, undressing, kissing, caressing. Mal took a hard seat on the bed, naked but for his socks. Meg stood over him, giving him his first glimpse of her new look. His breath caught as he looked at her pussy.

"You shaved."

She nodded.

"For him?"

She bit her lip, but nodded again. Mal's cock, already hard, thickened at the thought. He loved that look, but the fact that she'd done it for another man was equally arousing. What else was she willing to do?

Meg climbed into his lap. Her pussy was drenched, hot and wel-coming. "Uh, that's good," she groaned.

Mal couldn't agree more, but he couldn't vocalize it. He cupped her ass cheeks, guiding her up and down his shaft. She felt different in her smoother state. Like a stranger. Like Elena. He fucked her harder, the memory of Elena's naked body rolling across his imagination. He fucked Meg like he'd wanted to fuck that slut, using her body, tak-ing control of her. He squeezed her ass until he was sure he'd leave a hand print. His muscles burned with exertion. He fucked her like he hoped David would fuck her. On and on. Harder and harder.

Meg gave herself to him, relinquishing any control she had as Mal manhandled her. He didn't fuck her like this. Not normally. And normally, she preferred his softer, more attentive way. But right then, in that moment, with their jumbled emotions, with the weight of what Mal had done and what Meg planned on doing, she needed to be fucked like this.

Mal exploded inside of her just as she reached her own super-heated orgasm. She wrapped her arms around him, smothering him against her sweat-slick body. She could feel his heart race against her breasts. Could feel his heavy breathing wash across her.

She pushed her thick bangs out of her face, smiling as she looked down at her husband. "That was nice."

"Yeah," Mal said.

"Promise me something," she said.

"What's that?"

"Promise me that when you do get together with Elena, you do *that* to her."

"Who do you think I was imagining just now?" Mal said. It wasn't a full-truth, but it was close enough.

Meg batted her lashes and smiled. "And who do you think I was?"

"We're good, right?" Mal asked. "You're not upset about to-night?"

Meg nodded. "Based on what you just did to me, I'd say we're great."

"Good, because I plan on doing it to you every night until you leave."

Nine

The weekend was the usual blur of kids activities—Tae Kwon Do, soccer, playdates. And yet, even with all those activities in place, it was still bedlam in the house. Mal, as usual, took the lead with the kids, especially since Meg still had a lot of work to do to ensure that young Ms. Anderson, who had been caught stumbling out of the nightclub at 3:00am on Saturday, managed to keep her three film deal.

She and David had been texting back and forth about their client.

[Megan]: I see what you see in her.

She linked a picture of Melanie flipping off a photographer, one eye half shut, the other gleaming madly. At least it wasn't another crotch shot.

[David]: I think we've all seen what I see in her. Think she'll flash the mediator?

Meg laughed. Someone was definitely going to flash a bare snatch at David but it wasn't going to be Melanie.

[Megan]: God, I hope not.

[David]: I am willing to volunteer to be on panties patrol if you

want me to check her every morning.

[Megan]: Wow! I appreciate your willingness to sacrifice. But you
know, we probably won't even see her until Friday. She only needs
to be at the hearing for the conclusion.

[David]: I stand by my offer to check her everyday.

"Um, Meg?" Mal said. "Judging by your smile, I'm guessing
you've transitioned from working back to flirting with your boy toy,
so maybe you could help me with this?"

Darryl was covered in a full rainbow of paint and looked sheep-
ishly at his mom.

"What happened?" she asked.

Mal groaned. "You should see the dog…. Speaking of which, if
you have *him*…." he shooed the six-year old toward his mother. "…I
need to tackle and wash Rexi before PETA shows up on our doorstep
and protests our turning the dog in a living billboard for gay rights."

Meg laughed. It was always an adventure with kids.

*

And not just with kids as it turned out. Friday night had been
hot. Saturday night was even better. They'd made love—well, fucked,
while spooning. It was a position Mal loved since it gave him access
to his wife's entire front, her breasts of course, but he'd spent most of
his time exploring and massaging her bare pussy, ultimately making
her come by playing with her engorged clit even as he rammed her
from behind. And despite Meg's efforts to be mindful, she enjoyed it
too because having Mal behind her meant that she could let her mind
wander and imagine that it was David, rather than her husband, who
was filling her and fondling her and making her come.

When Mal joined her in bed Sunday night after giving Justin lights out, she was already naked beneath the covers. He joined her. They kissed and Mal could sense his wife was already quivering with excitement.

"What's gotten into you?" he asked.

"Nothing yet." A smirk. "I'm just jealous that you're going to be fucking Elena again tomorrow, when I haven't even…had a taste."

A taste. Mal couldn't help imagining his wife running her tongue along David's cock.

"Nothing might happen."

Meg snorted.

"Nothing is stopping you from, um, getting a taste tomorrow yourself. I mean, doesn't David deserve some warning about what you're planning to do to him in LA? So he can get some extra sleep or stock up on vitamins or something."

She chuckled.

"That's not a bad idea, honey," she replied. "Maybe I should…." She paused, a wicked gleam coming into her eye.

"What?"

"When are you seeing Elena?"

"Uh, well, my class is at 10:00, so I guess we'll, um, talk after?"

"So like 11:00, eh? So here's an interesting idea. How about at 11:00 I invite David into my office."

Mal groaned as he realized where she was going.

"And when Elena is—"

"Going down on you. I'll be going down on him. Do you think it'll turn you to on to know that while you're getting your dick sucked, across town another man will be shoving his cock into your wife's mouth?"

"Oh God, Meg."

She rolled onto her back and pulled him between her legs. He thrust instinctively, his prick finding its mark, disappearing into his wife, hot, wet cunt.

"It does turn you on! Good. You didn't tell me. Did that little whore swallow your come? I need to know what I should do for David."

Mal groaned again as he visualized his wife, on her knees, taking a heavy, sticky load all over her pretty face.

"You'd like that, huh, Meg, swallowing David's come?"

They were moving together faster now.

"Yeah, baby, I would. There are so many thing I want to do for him that I don't do for you. Shave my pussy. Swallow his come...."

Take it in the ass, Mal thought. He'd been thinking about doing that to Elena, now he had to think about David doing that to Meg. What kind of woman does that? Shaves her snatch, swallows, takes it in the ass.

"You're such a slut Meg."

"Hmm," she moaned. "A slut for David's big cock."

Big? How did she know?

"A slut for his big, hard cock," she added in a sultry whisper, as her climax washed over her.

Mal followed right away, his wife's words echoing in his ears

*

Meg groaned in frustration. Fucking Judge Nichols and his emergency hearing. It was now approaching 11:00am, and instead of getting his dick sucked in her office, David was off assisting Richie prepare a brief. Worse, if the judge wasn't satisfied, David would be called off the California trip. And still worse, back across town, Mal was probably about to get his dick sucked a *second* time by that little slut Elena. It just wasn't fair.

Meg chuckled ruefully. In truth, she doubted she'd have had the guts to make a move on David *in the office.* It was bad enough she, a married woman, was planning to seduce a junior associate while on business travel, but three thousand miles made the whole idea at least plausible. Even if she and David did have an extended dalliance, they'd always have to be very, very careful around the office.

She thought about that as well. Is that what she wanted? An extended dalliance? She wasn't sure. Probably not. She didn't want a relationship with David. She just, well, wanted to fuck his brains out for a few days. That really wasn't *that much* to ask, was it?

Meanwhile Mal was with Elena. God only know what that little whore was offering now. She could tell Mal was holding back on her. She didn't blame him. As long as it wasn't big stuff. She suspect that if she ever *did* hook up with David, there might be a few details she wouldn't share either. For example, she knew she'd probably never be completely forthcoming about it if David was as big as she suspected. No man, no matter how secure needs to be told that his wife just got railed by a horsecock.

Of course, she didn't even know if she'd like it. What if it was uncomfortable? Or even painful? She shuddered.

But what if it wasn't. What if it was…divine? What if it left her feeling fulfilled and satisfied like she'd never been before? What if it left her wrung-out and hungry for more? What if….?

"Oh God," she groaned softly.

She pulled her sticky fingers from her panties.

"Nice, Meg, real nice. Mal's getting his dick sucked again, you're jerking off by yourself in your office."

*

"That's it. Great work everyone. Now close your eyes. Feel your muscles relaxing. Sense the way the energy is flowing out into your limbs, and back into your core."

Mal patrolled the room. It was a large class, mostly stay-at-home moms, and though many were very cute, it made Elena stand out even more. Or maybe it was just that she was the only one of the group who had gone down on him that made her stand out.

As he approached her, she looked up and their eyes met. She looked down and he followed her gaze, to between her legs, where she dragged a finger across the tight fabric that exaggerated rather than concealed her cameltoe, both labia clearly outlined, the gap in between a hint at the deliciousness beneath.

He stumbled into the mat beside her.

"Oops, sorry," he muttered.

He looked back at Elena. She was grinning.

He finished up the class. As the students packed up, Elena approached. Mal looked around cautiously to make sure no one else was listening in.

"Hi beautiful," he said, trying to sound smooth. It was an act though. There was something about this young woman that unbalanced him.

"Hey, Teach. I wish you could have stayed longer Friday."

He smiled. "I had fun."

"Oh, I know you did. I did too. I love the taste of your come. I've been wanting a reminder of it for days."

Mal looked around anxiously. There would be another class coming in shortly.

She laughed. "Oh, don't worry, I have to run to class, and as much as I'd love to suck your cock again, right now, I'd rather not be distracted by the taste on my tongue while I'm in Torts. But I did want to schedule that private lesson…and I do mean private."

He nodded. "Um, sure…."

"Do you have time Wednesday?"

He thought about his schedule. *Sure. Drop my wife off at the airport so she can fuck another man, and then I'll drive back into town and bang Elena before picking up the kids from school. All perfectly normal.*

"Yeah. Late morning? 11:00?"

"Perfect. I don't have any classes Wednesday, so we'll have plenty of time."

She stepped in close.

"And we're going to need plenty of time, Teach, because after we get all hot and sweaty working on handstands, I'm going to strip you naked and lick every last drop of sweat off your hot body."

"Oh God," he groaned.

"I guarantee you'll be saying that when I tongue your ass. Has anyone ever done that for you? Does your wife?"

Mal shook his head.

"I'm going to rock your world, Teach. And then, you're going to fuck my tight little pussy until I scream. How's that for a *private* lesson?"

"I'll, uh, clear my calendar."

She grinned and gave his package a firm squeeze.

"You do that."

Once she left the room, Mal moved uneasily to the wall, leaning against it for support. His phone buzzed with income text.

[Megan]: My plans fell through. I hope you had more fun.

Mal was simultaneously disappointed and relieved. Hard to explain, but he was both dreading and anticipating the moment when Meg first experienced David.

[Malik]: Nothing happened. Just made plans for a private lesson later this week.

[Megan]: Sounds like we're both unlucky at love today. We'll have to make up for it tonight.

He smiled. Now there was a sentiment he could unambiguously get behind.

Ten

Meg felt all tingly. It was really going to happen. Nothing had happened yet, which did annoy her a little. The dueling blowjobs plan had fallen through on both ends Monday, but she was pretty sure Mal's "private lesson" would be the real deal. Damn that Elena was a self-confident little slut. And inspiring too. Meg and Mal had spent the last two nights playing around with the idea of licking all over. Well, not *all over*, but close. She looked at her watch. Yup. The private lesson was about to begin. She decided to put that out of her head. She'd get the play-by-play from Mal later.

In the meantime, here they were, side-by-side in business class, Meg and David, flying out to California for four days of their own *experimentation*. Not that she'd clued him in yet, but she'd caught him looking. Just a matter of reeling him in.

Maybe she could start right now. How cool would it be to begin their game with an introduction in the Mile High Club? She looked around. Hmmm, not that cool. Daytime trip. Almost full. Bathrooms cramped and uncomfortable, even if they didn't get busted by the flight crew. No, that idea would have to wait until she managed to get them onto a private jet. So the hotel it would have to be. Dinner, a couple of drinks, *hey David come by my room to review these documents before the start of the arbitration.* Of course, she did have to review documents, but no reason they couldn't do that naked between sessions of fucking like bunnies.

*

"I want my lesson in the nude," Elena said simply as she entered the smaller studio they used for private lessons.

Mal groaned. He'd expected that and had reserved the last studio on the hallway. The door was locked. But April, the owner, had a key. And the janitor had a key. And who knows who else?

"You know, someone could walk in on us," he cautioned.

She stripped off her top, exposing her lovely, pert breasts. "Are you trying to get me hot? Because," she continued, stripping off her yoga pants, "you don't need to do that. I'm already wet just thinking of your hot body. Want to see?"

She took his hand and moved it between her legs. His finger tips found her wet slit. She let out a soft, intoxicating moan.

"Now you get naked," she said.

He pulled his tee shirt up over his head. "Didn't you used to be shyer?"

She grinned. "Once I've sucked a man's cock, I no longer feel nervous around him. It's a trick I learned with a particularly intimidating teacher back in high school. It has served me well since. Now the pants, Teach. I want to see if your cock is as pretty as I remember it."

Mal shook his head ruefully. *This girl is trouble.* Delicious, delicious trouble. He stripped off the rest of his clothes. He looked in the mirror at the two of them standing side-by-side. Damn, they looked good together, barely an ounce of body fat between them. Mal always touted the health and mental well-being aspects of yoga, but the truth was, he loved the body it gave him, and the confidence being ripped provided. The confidence to strip naked in front of a sexy, young woman and know she'd like what she saw.

He watched her reach out and grab his cock, already swollen with excitement, but now completely hard at her touch. She was watching them in the mirror as well. Her nipples were swollen with excitement, her pussy glistening, everything about her exuding a hungry eagerness to fuck.

"What now?" he asked.

She gave his cock one last firm stroke. "You give me a lesson."

He led her through stretches and then a warm-up sequences of simple poses. He circled her, adjusting her posture with light touches. It was the same thing he'd do in any private lesson, but both of them being completely naked made it almost unbearably erotic. She too was obviously quite confident in her body, because in the various poses she was completely exposed, her tits, her pussy, even her cute, little, rosebud asshole. There wasn't an inch of her he hadn't seen up close.

He let his fingers graze across her skin, enjoying the little frissons his touch elicited. As he moved her into Downward Dog, he caressed her hard ass, then reaching between her legs to tease her hot, wet pussy. Then to Cobra, her legs flat against the ground, torso arched so that she looked up at him.

"Come closer," she urged.

When he did, she edged closer, and still in Cobra tickled his scrotum with her tongue. Mal was tempted to cup her head, feeding his prick into her willing mouth, but he was enjoying this yoga as foreplay too much to just go into right into sex. She seemed to feel the same way, smiling lewdly and waving her ass at him when he moved her into Cow, hands and knees, back arched.

"No wiggling. Hold your pose," he chided playfully.

It would be even more tantalizing to step in close and plunge his stiff cock into her pretty little pussy. He resisted though, instead contenting himself with running his hand over her ass, sliding a finger between her cheeks to tickle her anus. She moaned softly at his touch and didn't flinch, which Mal took as confirmation of his suspicion her butt was in play.

His restraint finally gave out when they moved to stands. With Elena executing a perfect Scorpion pose, balanced on her forearms, her body in the shape of a C, legs spread slightly to maintain balance, pelvis thrust out.

"Very nice, very nice," he intoned.

He kneeled down before her and reached around to support the arch of her back, pulling her pussy toward his face in the process.

"Now, let's test your ability to focus. How long can you hold the pose when I do this?"

He leaned forward and ran his tongue down her wet slit.

She swayed a little in surprise, but impressively held the pose.

"You have an interesting way of teaching yoga," she giggled.

"Quiet. Stay focused," he instructed.

He licked her again, more firmly this time, his tongue snaking between her lips, tasting her tangy juices. The tip of his tongue found her swollen clit. She gasped. He sucked it into his mouth. She gasped and trembled and then suddenly lost her balance. He caught her and eased her down.

"You need to work on your concentration," he noted dryly.

She chuckled. "Oh, yeah? Let's see you do better."

He grinned and then smoothly moved into a perfect handstand.

"Impressive," she said, "very impressive."

She circled him like a predator, licking her lips in anticipation, her fingertips trailing across his taut abs, his hard ass. She moved in front of him. He caught just a glimpse of her glistening snatch through his arms, and felt rather than saw her swallow his hard prick into her hot, inviting mouth. She swirling her tongue around his shaft as she bobbed up and down on his prick, faster and faster, deeper and deeper until her lips were nuzzled against his closely cropped pubic hair. Still, he remained in a perfect handstand.

"Even more impressive," she commented as she let his cock slip from her mouth.

She moved around him. He felt her hands on his ass, pulling his cheeks apart. He tried to clear his mind. *Focus on the pose.* But it was fruitless. The moment her tongue began flicking at his ass he began to shiver. And when she continued to probe, trying to work her tongue inside, he lost it, collapsing onto the mat flat on his back.

He looked up at her, standing over him, legs slightly spread, grinning. "You need to work on your concentration. But not right now. Because right now, you're going to shove that gorgeous cock of yours into my hot, wet snatch."

"I thought I was in charge here," he replied.

"Not anymore."

She walked over to her bag and removed a condom. She tore open the pack and deftly rolled it down over his prick. Feet flat on the ground, she squatted down and without ceremony impaled herself fully on his cock.

"Fuck, I love that feeling," she cooed.

Mal had the same thought, but he was too overcome for a moment by her frank sexuality to speak. Then she began to ride him, squatting up and down rapidly as she expertly worked his prick with her twat. It was an amazing view, seeing himself disappear into her over and over, his cock squishing inside her.

He reached out and place his right hand on her flat abdomen, his thumb dipping down to find her clit. She groaned.

"That's it, Teach, rub my hard little clitty while I fuck your cock."

He started off slowly. Meg often found it too much to have her clit rubbed during sex, but Elena, he realized…there probably wasn't any such thing as *too much* in her sexual vocabulary. He pressed down harder.

"Oh yeah, Baby, that's it, that's it…. oh God, you're making me come. You're making me come."

She gasped and then impaled herself once again hard onto him. Her felt her tight pussy spasm on his cock, and then she faltered and collapsed onto his chest.

He laughed. "See, you're still not keeping your focus."

He rolled them over and climbed off her.

"Now, I'm back in charge," he said. "Get into Cow."

Elena complied quickly, flipping over and getting on her hands and knees, back arched, ass high.

He edged in behind her and hammered his prick back into her snatch. She groaned and dropped her head. He reached out and grabbed a handful of her hair, yanking back.

"Head up, Elena, head up in Cow."

But even after she lifted her head, he didn't release his grip. Instead he yanked harder. She let out a lusty growl. Of course she'd like it rough. He lifted his other hand and brought it down firmly on her hard ass. She yelped excitedly. He noticed her asshole winking at him with each thrust. He remembered what Rod had done to Tammy. Mal licked his thumb and pressed it firmly into her butt.

That was it for Elena. She couldn't hold the pose any longer. Her shoulders sagged, her ass swaying back and forth. She was close he could tell, but he was closer.

"Oh God," he groaned.

"You had better not waste that load of come in a rubber. I want it in my mouth."

Double Oh God.

He pulled out, rose to his feet. She spun around quickly. He yanked off the condom just as he began to spurt. She opened her mouth wide, ropes of come firing out onto her cheeks and forehead.

"Your aim sucks," she complained.

"It looks pretty good from here," he replied, admiring how well he'd coated her face even if he had missed her mouth.

She harrumphed.

He tossed her a towel and she wiped her face.

"We'll have to do this again," he said. "I still haven't taught you to do a handstand."

She smiled and placed her palms on the ground. With practiced ease she rose up into a perfect handstand.

"Sorry, Teach, I guess you'll have to find something else to teach me."

Mal chuckled. He was pretty sure it would be the other way around.

*

Meg turned off airplane mode as they touched down in LA. There was a text from Mal.

[Malik]: Let me know when you land. And, babe? Show the young man a good time tonight.

She glanced over at David sitting beside her and blushed. What would he think if he knew she and her husband were texting about fucking him?

[Megan]: You know it. You and Elena had fun?

[Malik]: You have no idea. She's insane.

[Megan]: I'll call in a little to say goodnight to the kids. And then…well, let's say I'll be busy.

She looked against over at David, who turned and gave her a slightly awkward smile.

He knows. And he's a little scared. Good.

*

Meg got into her room and checked her email, and of course, a work crisis had developed while they were in the air. Solvable, but a few hours of effort.

They had adjoining rooms, Meg had made sure of that personally, and when he knocked to invite her down to dinner she gestured at her phone.

Oh, Okay. I'm going to get a bite to eat. He mimed at her.

She was a little disappointed that he didn't wait for her, but on the other hand, it was probably best if he was properly fed given what she had planned for him tonight.

One crisis let into another. But finally she got it all sorted out. She looked at her watch. 9:30pm LA time. Past midnight back home. She hadn't heard anything from David in a while, so she hoped he wasn't asleep already. Oh well, if she had to, she was fine with waking him.

Meg hopped into the shower. She cleaned up her pussy until she felt smooth and silky to the touch. Then standing naked before the mirror she dried her hair and put on her makeup. She was done with the games. She'd been waiting for this for too long. They could play dress up with her lingerie later. Tonight she was just going to knock on his door, and when he opened, drop her bathrobe and invite him in. And if he turned her down…well, he had better not.

She knocked on his adjoining door softly. No answer. Then louder. Still no answer. She called him. She heard his phone ringing from next door. Maybe he'd left it in the room when he went down to dinner? But that was over two hours ago. Maybe he was getting a post-dinner drink. Whatever, sooner or later he'd return, and then, hmmm, would she first suck his cock? Or have him go down on her? She liked the idea of the latter, but she also knew she wouldn't long be able to resist the curiosity of finding out for sure what was in his pants.

She knocked again at his door. Still nothing. She sighed. Since the kids had been around, Mal hadn't given her any details about Elena, but between the texts and what he did say, it was obvious those two had taken it to the next level already. Meg was antsy to start on her own experimentations.

Meg grabbed some documents and pulled a chair over by the door to David's room. Might as well do a little work until he got back.

She'd just finished off reviewing the file when she heard a sound from next door. She looked at her watch. 11:00pm. *Finally.* A little late, but better late than never. She put away her files and freshened herself up. She raised her fist to knock on the door when she heard it—a giggle. Unmistakably a woman's giggle. The TV? She pressed her ear to the door. No. She could hear muffled voices of two people, a man and a woman. Then a moan.

There is no way this is happening. He'd picked up a woman in the hotel?

But it was happening. The moans progressed to gasps and groans. Sheets being torn off the bed, a squeaking box spring. The woman's cries getting louder and louder.

"Oh my God! Oh my God! Oh my God!"

More grunts, groans. Then quiet. And then fifteen minutes later it started up again.

Meg sat down heavily on her king sized bed and stared at the door to David's room. *You have to be shitting me.*

*

[Malik]: *So did the young man have a good time last night?*

[Megan]: *He sure did.*

[Malik]: *Great!*

[Megan]: *And so did the woman he was with.*

[Malik]: *Um, that was you, right?*

[Megan]: *I wish.*

*

She scolded him at breakfast. "We are not here on vacation you know."

"I'm sorry, I just thought we were all ready and—"

"From now on, David, you clear it with me if you're going to go out and socialize."

"Yeah. Wow. Okay, Megan. I'm sorry."

She felt bad when he walked away to reload his breakfast plate. But fuck it, she hadn't flown his sexy ass out to California so he could fuck other girls.

She chuckled to herself. Based on how much he was eating, he'd burned a lot of calories last night. There was some good news. Judging by how many times he'd made his guest scream in passion, the kid was a real studmuffin. Now it was just a matter of getting his big prick aimed in the right fucking direction.

Eleven

To say that Mal was distracted was an understatement. Elena in the front row had something to do with it. She wore her bright pink tank top with her cropped black pants—one of her more modest outfits, but still killer—and kept smiling at him whenever he looked her way.

But also, he thought of his wife on the other side of the country, and how she'd spent last night alone. Part of what helped him deal with his guilt at screwing around with Elena was that Meg was getting something herself. Except she wasn't.

Class finished up. Elena hung back, looking so tempting as she sidled up to him. Guilty or not, she had his heart racing.

"Hey, Teach. You doing anything?"

He knew that all he had to say was, "No," and they'd be fucking again, and as tempting as that was, he didn't think Meg would be thrilled about it, experiment or not. "I've got some errands to run, actually."

If Elena was disappointed, she didn't show it. She just smiled, bounced on her heels, and said, "Maybe another time."

Mal watched her leave with no small amount of regret. He almost changed his mind and chased her out into the parking lot. Instead, he just watched her climb into her little Civic and drive away.

He didn't even get a backwards glance.

Mal considered that. He considered himself a pretty casual guy, and back before he was married, he had his fair share of casual encounters. Elena's attitude was no different than he would have been back in the day, but it just felt so foreign now. Was that what it would be like for Meg, if she managed to get into David's pants?

*

"That was impressive," David said. They were having an early dinner at a restaurant by the courthouse, celebrating a successful first day. "You were prepared for everything that was thrown at you. Did you even look at your notes?"

"I looked," Meg said with a smile. She was in high spirits, too. Today wasn't a trial, it wasn't litigation, but it was still her in a courtroom out-arguing the other councelor. It always gave her a rush. "That's why it's important to do your homework. I spent most of last night reviewing everything once again."

David had the decency to look embarrassed. She liked that she'd put that slight flush in his cheeks. "I'm sorry about last night."

"Sounded like you were having fun." Meg felt the same spike of adrenaline that she felt when arguing a case.

David met her eyes steadily. "Oh, I was."

Meg kept her cool, although her breath came slightly shallower and heat boiled under her dress. She reached for a glass of wine, happy to see that her hand was steady. Picking it up, she raised it to David. "Then here's a toast...to successful preparations for tomorrow."

Uncertain if this was a test or not, David picked his glass up, clinking it to his boss's. Meg saw that he was off-balance. She pressed on while she still had the advantage. "So how did that work?" she asked. "You and Ms. Last Night?"

"What do you mean?" He looked very uncomfortable.

"I'm just trying to understand it. You went downstairs for some food, and then you're bringing back a little dessert." She heard the jealousy in her voice and squashed it. Hopefully David was too busy coming up with the right response to give his boss to notice.

"I went down to the hotel restaurant to get some dinner, but didn't immediately order because I was waiting for you. I sat at the bar, waiting, watching the baseball game—they've got this huge television in the lounge…. Anyway, while I was sitting there, this… woman joined me."

"She have a name?"

"Erica." He watched her watch him and something in his demeanor shifted. He stopped shifting. He straightened his back ever so slightly, rolling his shoulders back. "It was her last night in LA and she was feeling lonely."

"So you kept her company. How noble of you."

"I know, right?" He smiled. "I was only doing my duty as a gentleman. Seriously though, I was waiting for you."

"And when I didn't come down?"

"I figured you were probably caught up in something. Or you'd fallen asleep. So Erica and I had some dinner, we went back to the bar, then…back up to my room."

Slut, Meg thought, even as she acknowledged the duplicity to herself. "When did you get to sleep?" she asked.

"I'm not sure. Late?"

"So do you offer the same hospitality to all the lonely ladies you meet?" Meg asked, feeling her blood pressure rise.

David looked at her as if trying to decide whether the suggestion in her question was imagined or not. His eyes moved into her cleavage before he answered. "Only the hot ones."

"Now that doesn't sound very chivalrous."

"Don't worry, you don't have to worry about it," he said.

Meg felt the air between them thicken. She felt drunk, despite having only had a few sips of wine. "What makes you think that I'm not lonely?"

David met her eyes, his hesitation feeling more calculated than uncertain. "Not what I meant, but that's interesting to know."

You're one of the hot ones, he didn't need to say. Meg heard it, loud and clear.

"I hope you're not going to be upset, but after dinner, I was thinking that we need to go over the case one more time. Since Melanie Anderson's going to be appearing tomorrow, and who knows what she might do or say…."

"We should be prepared for anything." The way he looked at her made her toes curl in anticipation. "Great idea."

*

Meg's heart was racing when she stepped inside her hotel room. She was alone, but not for long. Not this time. David had swung by his room to grab his laptop. They were still operating under the pretense that this was a working session.

"You can do this," she whispered to herself. It helped that Mal had already slept with Elena. That gave her motivation to even up the score, at the very least.

Meg pulled the suit's jacket off and closed the closet door, which was entirely made up of mirror. She checked herself out, making sure her hair was still in place. Without the jacket, her pinstriped dress suit was almost sexy—tight, sleeveless, and relatively short for a business suit. Her hair was still up, contained in a copper-hued bun, and her make-up was understated but impeccable. She would have liked to have had more time to retouch it, but it would do.

The knock came at the adjoining door. Meg took one last, fortifying breath, then opened the door.

David still wore his shirt and trousers, although he'd left his jacket in his room, and his tie was long gone. He didn't have anything with him. No laptop. No satchel. Not even a pen to take notes with. Beyond that, though, there was something different about him. Something that Meg couldn't quite place.

"Forget something?" she asked.

"Right. My laptop." The door clicked shut behind David. "I can go back and get it if you want to keep playing that game."

Meg took a step back before she could help herself.

"Or we can play something more fun."

He was cute enough that the presumption didn't come off as arrogant, but where she'd once seen charm in that dimpled smile, she couldn't help seeing something more sinister...and exciting.

She almost denied it—the good girl in her acting out. She almost put a hand on her chest and said, *I don't know what you're talking about.*

But she didn't. The memory of her sitting alone on her bed last night, listening to David pound some girl into submission, was too vivid. So she raised a brow and said, "What did you have in mind?"

David took a step toward her. Again, she took a step back before she could help herself. This time, it brought her against the closet door. David pursued, invading her personal space. She could smell his musk beneath his cologne—so different than Mal. She could feel his heat. Yet he didn't touch her. Not yet.

"Last night, I kept waiting for you to join me. You know how disappointed I was when you stood me up?"

"I didn't stand you up. I was working...." Suddenly, she felt like a schoolgirl, searching for excuses. She found her more confident side. "And you seemed to get over your disappointment pretty quick."

"Are you going to keep holding that against me?"

"Depends on how far you're willing to go to make it up to me."

"Oh, I was planning on going pretty far," he said. His insinuation went straight down between her thighs. She pressed herself harder against the closet door, feeling the cool mirror against her palms. David closed the distance, his lips finding hers.

The moan that emerged as he kissed her was almost a whine. Instinctively, her hands went to his torso, prepared to push him away. Instead, they curled into fists, clutching him close as she opened her mouth to his invading tongue.

He did not kiss her like Mal. It wasn't just that he was unfamiliar. He was just more...aggressive. Their tongues didn't simply play and tease—they fought for the upper hand, fencing, fighting, pursuing.

As they kissed, their hands roamed, exploring one another for the first time. Meg traced the contours of his back, his sinewy muscle thicker and harder but just as sexy as she'd imagined when riding behind him at the gym. His ass was nice, too, she admitted, although nothing would beat her husband's body. It was his cock that she so desperately wanted to touch—so of course she denied herself. At first.

David palmed her tits, squeezing them harder than her husband would, but in a good way. He knew what he was doing. These weren't the boyish fumblings of a nervous young man. Then again, after what she'd heard last night, she knew that he wasn't.

When she felt his hands leave her tits and travel lower, she knew that this was her last chance to stop him. Once he had his hands under her dress, she wouldn't be able to stop.

"I've always liked this suit," he said, breaking the kiss momentarily. "And I've always wanted to do this."

He looked down her body as he pulled the pinstripe suit up her legs, revealing her black stockings and the snaps of the garter belt holding it in place.

"You naughty, naughty woman," he grinned.

"It gives me confidence in the courtroom." It wasn't totally true, but she liked the idea of David thinking that she always wore something sexy under her suits. Based on his smile, he seemed to buy it, and that, in turn, gave her the confidence to do the next thing. "You can start making things up to me right about here."

She placed her hands on his shoulders and pushed him down. This was the moment she'd been dreaming about, the powerful executive boss making her shy employee submit to her. Somehow, David and his wolfish grin didn't give her the satisfaction, even as he knelt down before her. Somehow, the young man made the humble action seem like his idea.

"I've always wondered if you were a natural redhead," he said. He pushed his hands up under her skirt, grasping her thong. When he pulled it down, she was pleased to see the look of surprise in his eyes.

"I am, but you won't find the evidence there," she said.

He touched her cunt, brushing his thumb across her shaved mound. "Even naughtier," he said, licking his lips as he looked up at her. "Let me guess. This gives you confidence in court, too?"

"Mostly with young, junior attorneys."

"I can't wait until I fuck you," he said. Without another word, he buried his face between her thighs and closed his mouth over her pussy. Just like the kiss, he was more forceful, going right for his clit with his tongue. Meg was glad that she had the wall behind her to keep her steady.

She closed her eyes, rocking her head back as he worked her. Her fingers raked through his thick hair, yet another reminder that this wasn't Mal between her legs. This was happening. This was really happening. *I can't wait to fuck you….* She shivered. She couldn't wait, either.

He pushed two fingers inside, curling them up against her g-spot. Pulling back, he said, "You know I see you looking at me, don't you?"

Meg shivered, afraid to answer. Her heart palpitated. He knew?

"I see you looking. Wondering." He fucked her with his fingers. "Do you play with yourself, thinking about me?"

Meg moaned. David leaned in, flicking her clit rapidly before backing off again. She protested before he said, "Tell me, Meg? Have you played with this shaved pussy, thinking about me?"

She nodded.

"Say it," he said.

Her answer was short. Breathless. "Yes."

"When you're with your husband, do you think about me fucking you?"

"Yes." The confession felt terrible and sexy all at once. She opened her eyes to look down at him. He was there, looking up at her from between her legs, two fingers twisting in and out of her.

"And in these fantasies, are you a good girl?"

"N-no…."

He rose, his fingers still inside of her, still fingering her.

"I didn't think so." With his left hand, his free hand, he grabbed her by the hair and yanked her head back. She cried out, but didn't move to stop him. "You were dirty, weren't you? You imagined yourself doing things with me that you don't do for him. Don't you?"

"Yes," she hissed.

He kissed her exposed neck, up under her chin, before drawing her lips to his for another hard kiss. She tasted herself. That felt naughty, too, and she didn't dare protest.

"Take off your clothes."

The order took the breath out of her. He stepped back, removing his fingers from her at last. He didn't move to do the same. He just leaned on back on the opposite wall of the hall, crossed his arms, and watched. Where had the young junior attorney gone?

Meg met his eyes steadily, once again reminding herself who she was. She was his boss. She also got the feeling that he liked a little power struggle.

Reaching behind her, she unzipped the dress and shrugged out of it. With her thong gone and her pussy framed nicely by her garter belt, she felt the urge to cover up. She didn't.

"That's a sexy bra, but I've been dying to see those tits of yours. Take it off."

Again, her chest tightened at the authority in his voice. Again, she sought to turn things to her advantage, forming a smile on her lips that said, *I'm doing this for me, not for you.*

Carefully, she unclasped the bra and peeled it off, gathering her breasts in her hands, covering them for one last moment of modesty. "You like big tits, David?"

"Sure. What guy doesn't?" he said.

"I've seen you looking, too, you know," she said. She squeezed her heavy breasts. "Have you fantasized about these?"

"You know it."

She moved her palms lower, revealing the caps of her nipples. They were screaming and hard. "Do they make you hard?"

"Everything about you makes me hard."

"Show me."

David grinned. With cool nonchalance, he started unbuttoning his shirt. Unlike Mal, his sculpted upper body was hairless, although it didn't detract from his masculinity. She swirled her fingers around her nipples. He watched her watch him.

"Know what I can't wait to do with those?" he asked. Just as casually, he unbuckled his belt. The clink of it sent shivers through her. Unbuttoning his trousers, he quickly unzipped himself before pausing. "I can't wait to wrap them around my cock. Those puppies are practically begging to get fucked."

With that, he lowered his pants and unleashed the largest cock that Meg had ever seen.

"Oh, wow...." she said before she could help herself. It wasn't even fully erect and it was bigger than Mal's. Shaved bare, too, which only made it look larger.

David grinned. He knew what he had, and he clearly understood the effect that it had on women. "Your turn to get on your knees, Meg. Come here and suck it."

Meg did as she was told, not caring how she was behaving. She'd been thinking about this for too long for her to do anything else. That the reality actually surpassed her imagination made him irresistible.

She couldn't take her eyes off of it as she sank to her knees, and when she reached out to touch it, she could barely wrap her fingers around it. Incredibly, it began to grow at her touch.

"Go ahead and give it a little kiss," David said. She didn't look away from it. Instead, she leaned in and gave it a tentative lick. It grew some more. "Yes, Meg. That's a good little slut. Show me what you can do."

At last, she glanced up at him. Saw that smug look. Saw the challenge. She tightened her grip and swallowed him.

Jesus, he was huge. He filled her mouth before she could even take half of him. She pumped him like that, making sure to get as much saliva working as she could, before going deeper. Froth drooled down the base of his shaft. She jacked it in with her pumping hands, each working in harmony.

"That's it, Meg. Swallow me. Show me what you've got."

He was pushing her buttons and she knew it. It didn't matter. She relaxed her throat muscles and swallowed him into her throat. He gasped, his mouth going open, his eyes narrowing in pleasure. That reaction alone was worth it. She pulled back, jacking him vigorously.

"Like that?" Her voice was hoarse. She didn't wait for an answer, returning to all that hard meat. Again, she took it into her throat, longer this time. Deeper.

"Oh, fuck, baby. Oh, fuck yeah."

His words had their intended effect—not just encouraging her, but setting fire to her pussy. She owned him. Owned this man and his colossal cock. He may have found some slut last night, but this is what he really wanted.

His fingers threaded into her hair, unraveling the bun. "Fuck, you've got a great mouth," he said. "Can you take more?"

Before she knew what was happening, the fingers in her hair tightened. He guided her head along his length, gently at first, then with more force. She grunted in protest. Tried to set her own pace. David wasn't having any of it.

"Uh, uh, Meg. You might be the boss back home, but we're thousands of miles away from all of that." He thrust his hips forward, pushing more of his cock into mouth than she was ready for. She gagged. He pulled back, letting her breathe. "Here, you're my slut. Understand?"

She should have been angry. She hated when Mal did what he

was doing. Normally, she hated the loss of control. But with David, she got so hot. She heard his words, and they set fire to her body.

"Do you understand, slut? Say it."

He face fucked her harder. Saliva frothed and drooled down her chin, dripping onto her tits. "Mmm hmm," she gurgled around his erection.

He yanked his cock from her mouth. "Show me what you can do with those tits."

Meg straightened up on her knees. Hefting her tits in her hands, she wrapped them around his erection. She'd done this with a few boyfriends, back before Mal, but never since. It didn't matter. David knew what to do and immediately took control. His hands covered hers as he bent his knees and started to fuck her tits.

"I've wanted to do this from the moment I saw you, Meg." His cock speared through her cleavage, bursting out of the top, purple, swollen, and tempting. "And you know what? I knew I'd have you. I knew you had it in you. The way your eyes always lingered on my cock...and I gave you plenty of opportunities to stare, didn't I?"

"Yes." He'd set her up.

"You ready to feel this inside of you?"

Oh, God, was she?

"We can stop now if you want."

"No. Please...."

"Tell me what you want." He kept sawing away on her tits, never slowing, tantalizing her with a view of his cock.

"I want you to fuck me."

"I know you can be dirtier than that."

"I want you to fuck me with your...cock."

"Dirtier," he ordered. "Or I can just go call up Erica again. I'm sure she'd be ready to go—"

"I want you to fuck me. I want you to use me. I want your big, hard cock to stretch out my slutty, married pussy until I scream. Can you do that? Are you man enough to do that?"

David pulled his cock from her tits and traced it along her neck, over her mouth again. She went to take it back into her mouth, but he pulled it away. "Only one way to find out," he said. "There's a condom in my pants. Get it out."

As she dug around for the foil wrapper, David finally moved out of the hallway, butt naked. God, he looked good. Not as ripped as Mal, but there was something sexy about the difference.

She rose to her feet, catching her reflection in the hall mirror. Stripped down to all but her black garter belt, stockings, and heels, her hair wild and uncontained, she could barely recognize herself. Was this the same, respectable attorney who'd kicked ass earlier? Was this the mother of three?

"Yeah, you do look good," David said, misinterpreting the way she was looking at herself.

He was standing by the bed, his hand idly stroking his cock. Its size sent a tremor through her. Could she fit that inside of her? Would she like it? *You do look good*, he'd said. She rolled with that, regaining the confidence that she normally commanded. Whoever she was before or after this moment, tonight, she was David's, and David wanted her.

"Want some?" he asked. She didn't need him to clarify what he was talking about. She licked her lips and closed the distance between them.

They kissed again, heavy and hard. He was tall—taller than Mal—and she was happy that she was wearing the taller of her heels. Even still, he had to bow his head to meet hers. She liked that. It felt like a tiny victory.

She wrapped her hand around his cock. It was swollen to the point now where her thumb and forefinger couldn't actually touch. She sighed. So big.

David dominated her with the kiss, powering down into her until she could barely breathe. She tried to keep up with him, tried to ride it out, but when she started to feel smothered—when she was about to pull away—he did it for her. He didn't let her catch her breath, though.

Forcefully, he spun her around, pushing her down over the king-sized bed. The rooms here were luxury, with tall, raised beds. Even with her head against the mattress, the angle wasn't uncomfortable. She heard him tear open the condom wrapper. She held her breath, ready for what came next.

First, she felt his fingers again, two pushing inside her pussy. "You're so wet, Meg."

She wiggled her ass at him impatiently.

"Ready to get fucked?" he asked.

"Yes—"

Before the reply had fully left her lips, she felt him press into her. If anything, he felt bigger than he looked. Her world was reduced to the full sensation of David's cock as he entered her. She couldn't think of anything else. She opened her mouth, but no sound came out. She buried her face into the mattress instead, clutching the bed sheets in a white knuckled grip.

At last, she found her voice—a guttural scream that started loud and ended louder. It felt good to let that out. Felt like she'd unhitched herself from the last of her inhibitions. When she came back to her senses, her throat raw, David was still behind her, his gargantuan cock still buried inside her, and now, at last, she was ready to embrace it.

"How does that feel, Meg?" He didn't ask out of concern. That wasn't empathy in his voice. It was rhetorical, but she answered like it was.

"Big."

He withdrew. Even with the condom on, she felt every bump and ridge of him. She realized that he'd only just penetrated her, and she was already on the brink. "Let's get you used to the size. Then we can really fuck."

Meg nodded, liking the idea. When he pushed into her again, just a little faster than the first, her brain went up in flames all over again. He withdrew. Pushed inside. Another grunt. Another moan. Another brush with madness. Again and again, each thrust coming faster. Harder. Fuller. Better. Until he was fucking her, his hips slapping her ass, his cock sending lightning bolts through her body with each thrust. She'd never get used to this feeling—it would never be something she'd call *comfortable*—but damn, it felt good. So, so—

"Good!" she screamed, feeling her orgasm envelop her. David palmed an ass cheek, squeezing it hard enough that he had to have left a mark. She gave into the control, into the roughness. With Mal, she would have protested. With David, she wished he'd do more.

"That's it, Meg. Come for me. Come for David," he ordered. Her climax tightened around her, cutting off rational thought. She moaned and screamed, aural fireworks that lit up her mind.

He didn't stop fucking her in the come down. Instead, he grabbed her by the hair and yanked back. Pain seared through her. She screamed. Maybe it was her state of delirium, but the pain actually felt good.

She arched her back as he pulled her hair until she practically faced the ceiling, her tits still planted on the bed. David crawled onto the edge of the mattress, scooting them along until he was fucking her doggy style. He leaned over her, his smooth, sweaty skin hot against her back, and whispered, "You like it rough, don't you?"

"Yes," she hissed. Things had started to tighten up inside her again, like a coiled spring, barely held in check.

"But I bet your husband doesn't treat you like this, does he?"

She shook her head, a bead of sweat trickling down her face. Guilt registered somewhere in the distance at the mention of Mal, but David's cock commanded all her attention.

"He doesn't treat you like a dirty whore, does he?"

"No."

He wrapped a hand around her throat. Fear and excitement rattled through her as he squeezed. She felt dizzy. Light-headed.

"Touch yourself," he said, his voice a buzz in her ear. "Play with your clit."

She pushed both hands beneath her, finding her clitoris sensitive and swollen. She normally hated being told what to do, but David ordered, and she obeyed. He pulled her head back by the throat, bowing her back as he plowed her. She was his plaything. His fuck toy. His slut.

"Come. Now."

He may as well have pulled a trigger. Her second orgasm eclipsed the first. The lack of oxygen coupled with all the other stimuli turned her brain and body to mush. She may have screamed. She may have lost consciousness. She may have blacked out. One minute, David was riding her hard, the second, her throat was raw and her body was shaking.

David flipped her. Slid up over her, his body glistening with perspiration. His dark hair was matted, hanging around her face. He reminded her of Tarzan for a moment, here to snatch her and drag her back into the jungle. Instead, he speared her again, splitting her open with his still-rock hard cock.

Instinctively, she wrapped her legs around his back as he pounded her. He bent down and kissed her, sloppy and wet. Unlike before, there was desperation in that kiss. He was close, too, his control slipping. She seized the moment.

"That's it, David, fuck me. Fuck me like you've always wanted to."

"Uh, Meg." He groaned, his hips going into overdrive.

"That's it, baby. Show me how much you want it."

He powered into her. "I'll show you, you slut. I'll show you exactly what I think you deserve."

He pushed up until he was in a kneeling position, scooped one hand under her ass, and reached out and palmed a heavy, jiggling tit, and *fucked* her. Each long thrust broadsided her g-spot. She was once again gone after three strokes. Ten strokes, and he joined her.

She felt his cock pulse, expanding and contracting as he filled his condom. A dark part of her brain wished she could have felt his heat instead, but that dark part was silenced as her final orgasm of the night closed over her. This time, when she passed out, she was *out*.

Twelve

Mal groaned and looked again at his phone on the bedside table. Nothing. It was now after 4:00am and he hadn't slept a wink. He slammed down the phone in frustration, then chuckled to himself darkly. *It isn't the fucking phone's fault she hasn't called.*

He hadn't thought too much of it when Meg didn't check in early last night. True, she almost always called around the kids' bedtime when she was travelling, but okay, that was still the middle of the afternoon in LA so she was probably still working. Mal hadn't texted because he knew she'd call as soon as possible. Except, she hadn't.

By the time Mal sent his first text it was 10:00pm.

[Malik]: Hey babe, hope you had a good day today. Big plans tonight?

He was expecting a quick reply, an apology for having missed her usual evening call and maybe a flirty update about her plans with David. Mal was discovering that was part of the fun of the game for him, that weird mix of jealousy and arousal that came each time he thought of his wife with her new crush.

At midnight, another text.

[Malik]: You must be busy. ;-) What's going on?

Still nothing. Okay, so she was with *him*. And they had work tomorrow, so whatever happened, it would surely be an early night. He'd be getting a text, or better yet a call any minute now.

By 2:00am, Mal's mood darkened. Where the hell was she? He was tempted to send another text, but didn't want to appear needy. He now regretted spurning Elena's latest advance. Not that it would have particularly eased his anxiety over his wife, but it would have been a distraction. Not really fair to use Elena that way, but then again, Elena didn't seem like the kind of girl to get easily attached. Mal was under no illusion that Elena saw him as anything other than a sport fuck. He smiled. *There are worse things in life.*

Fuck needy. At 5:00am he sent her another text.

[Malik]: *Guess you must be asleep by now. Let me know how it went.*

Mal felt there was something vaguely pitiful about knowing his wife was with another man and being reduced to begging for scraps of information. He wondered if she really was asleep or whether she was still with him. Had they been fucking all this time? Were they still at it? Was David's cock churning inside Meg's juicy pussy even now? Was she showing him the texts while they screwed? Talking about responses, joking about him until Meg, lost in passion, turned off the phone to focus all her attention on the sensation of another man inside her....

At 9:00am he sent his last text.

[Malik]: *I know you're having fun, but you missed the kids last night and this morning. I'm going to work now.*

*

Meg's alarm woke her at 7:00am. She felt sore all over, between her legs from taking his big cock, the back of her head where he'd pulled her hair, her breasts from his rough handling. All little reminders of an epic fucking. She smiled. Sex with David had lived up to her every expectation, surpassed them even. *Did he really fuck me unconscious?*

Speaking of which, where was he? She was a little disappointed that he wasn't in bed with her, his sexy body pressed up against hers, his morning wood an invitation for a quickie before showering. Waking up alone made Meg feel a little used, but then again, that was a small price to pay for the experience.

She looked at the phone.

"Shit."

Mal. It wasn't so much that she'd forgotten about him. She'd meant to text *after*, and hadn't planned on being fucking into oblivion, but the truth was, she also wasn't thinking that much about him either. She'd make it up to him. When she got home, they'd reconnect, share their experiences, make love in the retelling. She smiled. God she loved Malik. Their life together, and now the gift of this experience. Oh sure, he was getting it on with that little whore Elena, but as Meg focused again on the throbbing between her legs, it occurred to her that she was getting the better end of the deal.

[Megan]: I am SO sorry. Things got a little crazy. I'll explain when I get home. And I'll definitely call the kids tonight.

*

Mal locked his phone in his locker at the gym. Having it with him all day was just going to make him crazy, and the last thing students want is a distracted, anxious yoga instructor. He found an empty studio and put himself through a sequence of poses.

For Mal, the spiritual elements of yoga had always been secondary to the physical. Yet, as he focused on his breathing, on the position of his body, on the flow from one pose to the other, he felt a growing sense of peace and calm. Problems receded, perspective returned. He wasn't thinking of Meg, not directly, his mind was focused instead on the exercise, but he could feel his frustration soften, his anger diminish. Control, mindfulness, acceptance.

He exhaled deeply with his final stretch and then gathered up his mat and his towel and went to the larger studio where his class was held.

Several of the students were already there, including Elena. She was back in her short tights and sports bra combo. She looked like the sort of girl who'd have an Instagram account to show off her hot body, but now that she was in law school, he suspected that even if she'd had one once, it would be deleted by now. He'd just have to take his own pictures if he wanted them for the memories. She noticed his appraising glance and blew him a quick kiss. He blushed. So much for control.

After class, she approached him.

"Hey Teach, how about a happy hour tonight?"

He grinned. "Happy hour, huh?"

"Happy hour and then a happy ending? Does that make it more attractive?"

"It does, but my wife is out of town—"

"Oooh, even better. You can stay out late and we can really get in trouble."

It was a little hard to imagine what she would consider trouble. Elena was a free spirit.

"I wish. Kids."

She gave him a pout.

"Elena, I'm really not blowing you off. I do want to get together, just tonight is hard."

"Blowing and hard are my two favorite words."

He groaned.

"Okay, but don't keep me waiting too long."

"Look, send me a text later this weekend and I'll see if I can get away, yeah?"

She nodded. "Okay. See ya."

He watched her walk away, a sexy swivel in her ass. She was doing it on purpose. She had to be. No one's ass moved like that unless it was deliberate.

*

Meg came out of the shower wrapped in just a towel and startled.

"Jesus, you scared me!"

David laughed. He was sitting on the bed in her room, already in his court attire. Damn he cleaned up well, and he wasn't too bad naked either.

"What are you doing?" she asked as she noticed him playing with her thigh high stockings.

"Just picking out what you should wear today."

"You went through my stuff?"

He nodded. "You *are* a naughty girl."

He held up her glass dildo. Meg felt her face flush.

"It's a little small," he noted.

She'd never thought so before, but indeed, compared to his prick it was.

"You shouldn't be going through my stuff."

He smirked. "It's okay. I'll make it up to you. I'll let you suck my cock."

She chortled. "Oh really?"

David unzipped his fly.

"Stop it," she hissed.

He didn't. Instead, he pulled out his prick, still flaccid, but despite that still huge. She didn't like the way this was going. He was presumptuous, rude, bordering on abusive...but also so sexy...and Meg found she couldn't tear away her gaze as he slowly stroked himself for her.

"We don't have time for this," she said desperately.

"Then you better get to work."

He patted the bed beside him, and Meg took a step in his direction before she could stop herself.

"Come on, Meg. You know you want it. A nice big sausage for breakfast with a hot cream chaser."

The thing was, she *did* want it. She wanted that big tool in her mouth. To feel it grow and harden inside her. To taste his salty precum, to sense his excitement building, to hear his moans of pleasure.

It's just an out of town fling. Once we get home, everything will go back to normal.

He patted the bed again, and this time Meg didn't stop herself. As she approached, he reached out and loosened her towel. It fell to the floor, and she climbed onto the bed completely naked, on her hands and knees, her head dipping down into his lap. She opened her mouth wide and swallow the tip of his cock. She took advantage of the mushiness to lick and taste him, to swirl her tongue around his glans, and kiss and suck his velvety skin into her mouth.

He reached between her thighs and traced a finger over her slit. And again, with a little more pressure, her pussy split open for him.

"A sign of a real slut is getting wet when you're giving head," he observed.

Her excitement fed his. His cock swelled, stiffened. She found it harder to do anything other than bob up and down on him, her lips stretched painfully over his bulk.

She felt something hard rubbing against her pussy, spreading her open. She gasped around his cock as the knobby tip of her dildo slid against her clit. Back and forth, back and forth, he teased her with the smooth, solid phallus

"That's it, boss, take it deep."

She swallowed him deeper, taking him into her throat. And as she did, her firmly pressed the dildo inside her.

Oh God! It came out as a muffled moan. She bobbed up and down faster on his big prick. He fucked her in time with the sex toy. Her slurping gasps mixed with the sounds of the glass dildo squishing into her pussy. It was like being with two men at once, the thought triggering an image. Mal and David on either side of her, using her hard. Switching sides. Taking turns. So hot, so dirty.

She felt a surge of heat spreading from her belly. She moaned around his cock as she came. His hand clamped down on the back of her head as he thrust upward.

"I'm already dressed for work, so you'll need to drink it all. I don't want any stains."

She looked up at him. Their eyes met. She felt his prick swell and begin to pulse. He shot his first load right into her throat. She nearly choked on it, but forced herself to breathe through her nose and managed to get it down. She rose up off his cock a little, keeping just the tip in her mouth. Her hand stroked his hard, pulsing shaft, milking every last drop of jism, and even after, she continued to suckle his prick until she was sure there was nothing left.

He grinned. "A perfect start to the day."

"Don't get used to it," she replied.

He smirked enigmatically, but didn't argue. Instead, he reached behind him on the bed and lifted up a suit.

"I want you to wear this."

She laughed and shook her head. "No way. That one is way too short."

*

It was a small window of sanity. All the kids were finally in the same school, which meant that afternoon pickup was a single stop. Mal got there a little early. It was a lovely day, so he sat on a bench outside the school and waited for the kids to arrive. For all the talk of women's liberation, Mal couldn't help but notice that today, as with most days, he was the only dad making the elementary school pickup. It shouldn't have, but it always felt a little awkward—the moms seeing him as something of an outsider, maybe even a threat.

That was *their* problem, Mal reminded himself…or maybe he was convincing himself. The truth was that even though he was intellectually comfortable with his wife making more than him, and even though he was willing—happy even—to shoulder the majority of the child care duties, he was not immune to the gravitational tug of social norms and expectations. Somehow today, those subtle pressures felt stronger. Maybe it was just that all of them were outside, standing in discussion clutches with him excluded. Or maybe it was the knowledge that his wife was across the country right now with her lover. Not that they'd be doing anything *right now*. It was the middle of the day after all.

*

Meg felt naked. Not only was the skirt too short and too tight, but at David's insistence she'd gone with thigh highs and no panties. She could periodically feel cool gusts of air conditioned air cooling her pussy, which was probably a good thing because despite the constant struggle to avoid flashing anyone, being so exposed was undeniably thrilling. David encouraged her excitement with his knowing glances, and the way he was continually *accidentally* brushing against her, his fingertips trailing over the exposed flesh of her inner thigh.

Thankfully, David was handling most of the hearing this morning. After yesterday's presentations, this morning was just about the arbitrator working through some implementation questions. From the issues he was raising, it seemed as if he was likely to rule in their favor. More good news.

They broke for lunch with an admonition to be back in session at 1:30. There was a crowded deli across the street, but they had enough time for a proper sit-down meal, so instead they went to a nice steakhouse a couple of blocks from the courthouse. Their work was basically done, so Meg agreed when David suggested they have a glass of wine with their meal. Still, it was another step outside her comfort zone. Meg normally never drank in the middle of the day.

She excused herself and went to the ladies room. She looked at herself in the mirror. It was still the same woman she'd always been, and yet, different. She wondered if other people could see it as well. Could see that she was no longer...or maybe no longer *just* Meg, partner in a law firm, mother of three, good, responsible Meg, but *also* now lusty and slutty Meg.

The door to the restroom opened. She gasped.

"What are you doing here?"

He crossed to her, kissing her hard. She felt her stomach flutter, her head spin. *No!* She broke the kiss.

"Someone could walk in!" she protested urgently.

"Then we have no time to waste."

He grabbed her around the waist and lifted her onto the sink. He stepped between her thighs, spreading her legs, causing her skirt to ride up. Her pussy gleamed with excitement.

"We can't."

But she didn't stop him as he quickly dropped his pants. He was already hard. She gasped again at his size. No matter how many times she saw it, his prick always took her breath away. With a practiced skill, he deployed a condom, and then pressed forward, sliding his cock into her wet snatch in one firm thrust.

"Oh God," she gasped.

He palmed the back of her head and pulled her into a lusty kiss. His cock began churning inside her hard and fast. No subtlety. Just a rough, urgent quickie. She glanced up at the door. They were completely out in the open. *Anyone could walk in on them.* It was that thought as much as the sensation of David's huge prick filling her so completely that set her off. She bucked against him, felt her pussy spasming on his cock, and a moment later, she felt his response. His dick swelled and pulsed as he too came.

He pulled out quickly and threw the used condom in the trash. Meg remained up on the sink for a moment, panting and in shock. He gave her a quick kiss on the cheek, surprisingly tender.

"Don't dawdle. Our food will be out shortly."

She nodded curtly, but still hadn't been able to move by the time he exited the bathroom. Finally, she hopped off the sink and smoothed her suit. She looked herself in the mirror and smirked sarcastically. *Yup, same old Meg alright.*

*

Meg walked back to their table a little gingerly. She thought her pussy could use a good soak and a rest, but looking at David self-satisfied grin, she realized neither was in the offing. Of course, she could just say *no*. Or could she? Back at home, yes, of course. But here, in LA, three thousand miles from home, on a Friday night? Not a chance. Despite the soreness she felt, the realization that she wasn't through with him, nor him with her, gave her a thrill.

She settled down at the table.

"You're crazy," she said.

He smiled. Damn, he had a nice smile.

"So are you. You just didn't know it."

She shook her head. "No. This is just a temporary thing for me."

He smirked, an arrogant, knowing smirk that suggested he thought he knew her better than she knew herself. Was he always this insufferable? She was tempted to get into it with him, but he changed the subject.

"So, have you ever met Melanie?" he asked.

She shook her head. "Nope. Just worked through her *people*."

"She hasn't made a successful movie in, what, six years? How does she still have people?"

"A pretty face and a big rack go a long way, I guess."

He grinned. She blushed.

"I was talking about *her*."

"You're prettier than she is."

Meg rolled her eyes. Melanie for all her misadventures was a world-recognized sex symbol. She was just Meg with three kids and a house in the suburbs.

"So I guess you won't be trying to pick her up?"

"Oh, I didn't say that. But I was just thinking how much fun I could have with the two of you. You ever do it with a woman?"

Meg laughed. "You wish."

"I do…. And you didn't answer my question."

"None of your business."

"That's a *yes*," he crowed triumphantly.

She shook her head at his gambit. "David, I was cross-examining witnesses when you were still in high school trying to get into your girlfriend's pants."

"I didn't bother with high school girls. I was fucking my English teacher. I've always liked older woman. They're so desperate and grateful."

Meg felt a surge of anger. Then she noticed his grin. Ball busting.

"Fuck you," she replied sweetly.

He raised his glass. "I'll drink to that."

*

The phone rang in the kitchen.

"Mommy! Mommy!" Angela shrieked as she ran to pick it up.

Mal grinned as, sure enough, after a perfunctory greeting, Angela got to the real reason for her excitement, an impassioned complaint about Justin hogging the computer. As both the middle child and the only daughter, Angela was perpetually aggrieved, and only Meg was really able to talk her down.

It took a few minutes, but visibly calmed she passed the phone to Darryl and then to Justin. Finally the receiver came toward Mal. He felt a weird trepidation as he prepared to speak to his wife.

"Hey," he said.

"Hey, yourself."

"So things going well?"

"We won our case!"

"Great, but you know what I mean."

Meg hesitated. "Yeah. Real well. Crazy actually."

"Oh?"

"Mal? It's hard to explain, you know. I promise I want to tell you everything, but I'd sort of like to do it face-to-face. Feels weird having this conversation over the phone."

Now it was Mal's turn to think. They'd said "no lies." But they'd never discussed how promptly the disclosures had to come. Still, it felt like she was holding back. It was unsettling.

"Okay," he replied finally. "Any plans for tonight?"

"Melanie invited us to a celebration party at Skyline."

"Oh, cool, a real Hollywood party! Sounds like fun."

Meg laughed. "I guess so. It's just…this is all so crazy…and…."

Another surge of uneasiness. But Mal knew what he had to say. What she expected of him and what she deserved. "Babe, as long as you're having fun, go for it."

She sighed in relief. "I love you."

"Love you, too. Call me tomorrow."

Mal clicked off the phone. Why was he so anxious? They were in this together. And he'd already had some amazing encounters with Elena. He had no right to feel jealous. But right or not, he felt something—a sense of looming dread. Nothing concrete, just this weird sensation that what he had with Elena was somehow different than what was going on between his wife and David.

His thoughts were interrupted by screams from the other room. Meg's calming influence over Angela had lasted all of fifteen minutes, and now they were back at each other's throats. Fucking kids. Luckily it was getting toward bedtime, a full two-hour process of baths, reading, and tucking in. But Mal relished the familiarity and familyness of it. Like yoga, it was comforting and relaxing.

It was 9:30 when he closed the door to Justin's room and was finally done. He poured himself a glass of wine. As he took his first sip, his phone buzzed with an incoming text.

[Elena]: Hey teach, s'up?

He chuckled. A little early for a booty call, but her evening had started early at the Happy Hour.

[Malik]: Not much. Just having a glass of wine.

[Elena]: Want company?

He hesitated. He did want company. But he couldn't leave the kids alone, which meant inviting her over. That seemed like a big deal. Or was it? Meg had traveled across the country and was spending days with her man....

[Malik]: Want to come over?

[Elena]: yummy.

*

Mal heard the soft rapping at the front door and hurried to open it up for Elena. In between sending his text and her arrival, he'd been in a state close to panic. What if the kids woke up and saw her? What if someone saw her arriving? It was all very stressful.

He opened the door slightly and ushered her in. He began to close the door behind her when she stopped him.

"Wait."

She giggled and reached back through the doorway, dragging

forward a pretty young woman with pale blond hair and dark blues eyes.

"You remember Zoe, right?"

Mal groaned. *Trouble. Delicious trouble.*

The two young women were, no two ways about it, drunk. And giggling. And very, very sexy. Elena was dressed in a tight little leather skirt with a sheer white blouse that seemed designed to show off her sexy, white lace bra beneath. Zoe was equally provocatively attired in a clingy black and white striped party dress. Both women had bare legs and spiky black heels.

"You two look like you're going clubbing."

Elena grinned. "We still might. Unless we get a better offer."

Zoe sidled over to Mal and drunkenly wrapped an arm around his slender waist. "You go. I've got all I need here."

Elena slapped her friend's ass hard. "Don't worry, you little whore. Teach is enough for both of us. Isn't that right, Mal?"

Mal swelled with pride at the vote of confidence, though inside he couldn't avoid feeling a little anxious at the task before him. Two beautiful, slutty woman nearly half his age. It was the kind of challenge he couldn't refuse, and yet couldn't be sure of meeting.

He took a gulp of his wine and noticed them looking at him eagerly.

"Um, you two want a drink?"

"Fuck yeah," cried Zoe.

Elena slapped her. "*Shut up,*" she hissed in a stage whisper. "*His kids....*" Then turning to Mal, she added, "Tell me where to get to the wine, and shove your dick in her mouth to shut her up."

"Yes, please," Zoe sighed.

"Let's go upstairs," he suggested to Zoe as he pointed Elena toward the kitchen.

Bringing these two girls into his and Meg's bedroom was probably not a good idea, but it was the only room other than the bathrooms with a lock on it.

"I'll be right up," Elena chimed as she disappeared to get wine for them.

He led Zoe upstairs. Could it really possibly be this easy? Where were girls like this back when he was single? He chuckled to himself. Thank God they weren't around, otherwise he'd have never settled down.

He shushed her as they passed the kids' rooms. Happily they were at an age where they didn't often wake up in the middle of the night. Still, he was relieved once he got Zoe into the bedroom. She stalked around the perimeter and then flopped onto her belly on their king sized bed. She propped her elbows on the bed and rested her chin in her palms.

"I want to see you naked," Zoe cooed.

Mal started to object. It was *his* house after all. But then he shrugged. *Whatever.* He peeled off his t-shirt. She whistled.

"Shhh! I am going to have to gag you."

She apologized, and then nodded at him to keep going. He slipped off his gym pants and then his boxer briefs.

"Dayum, you are ripped."

Mal blushed, although he loved the compliment. They never got old.

"What are you doing over there, you little slut?" chimed Elena from behind them.

She entered the room with a bottle of wine and three glasses.

"Just admiring the view," Zoe replied.

"It's even better close up," Elena said.

Zoe rose from the bed and approached Mal. Elena poured them

wine. Zoe leaned in close and kissed Mal's neck gently, her hand grazing against his rapidly hardening cock. She took a glass from Elena and drained half of it in a single gulp.

"Zoe has great tits. Show him."

Zoe put down her glass, and with a coquettish smile, hooked her thumbs in the shoulders of her dress and yanked down the stretchy material. She wasn't wearing a bra, and her breasts spilled out, surprisingly large. Not as big as Meg's, but then again Meg's gorgeous breasts would have looked freakish on the more petite and slender Zoe. They were high and firm, with delectable nipples the size and color of ripe raspberries.

Elena circled around her friend and cupped her breasts from behind. She kissed her shoulder as she tweaked the blonde's large nipples. Then without a word, she grabbed hold of the fabric and yanked it down, over Zoe's flat stomach and slim hips, letting it fall to the floor. She wasn't wearing panties either, and Mal could see that she too was fully shaved.

"Do you always go out like that?" he asked.

"Only when we go clubbing," Zoe replied.

That hit Mal like a ton of bricks. Did that mean that Meg would also be naked beneath her dress when she went out with David? The thought of his wife, bare assed, with her newly shaved pussy out partying was harder to deal with than the notion of her fooling around with her boy toy in a hotel room. It just seemed more outrageous, more dangerous. He imagined Meg twirling on the dance floor, flashing strangers, and then sitting on a couch in some dark club, making out with David, his fingers inside her, every stranger passing by thinking of his wife as a slut. It made him feel queasy, but also excited.

"Looks like it turns you on," Elena said. "Time to get to work bitch," she added, pushing Zoe down to her knees.

Zoe didn't hesitate, sucking Mal's cock deep into her mouth. She bobbed eagerly up and down on his stiff prick, her hands fondling his balls. Elena, standing behind her friend, quickly shimmied out of her clothes as well. She approached and kissed Mal firmly on the lips before leaning down to suck hard on his nipple.

"Ow!" he hissed as she bit down. He grabbed her by the hair and yanked her away. She gave him an amused smile.

She stalked around him and pressed up against him from behind. He could feel her hard nipples pressing into his back and she reached around and pulled him close. She kissed his muscular back, her lips following the line of his spine, lower, lower. On her knees behind him, she massaged and kissed his butt.

Mal looked around at the two beautiful young women kneeling at his feet, Zoe sucking him enthusiastically, and Elena kneading his ass, pulling apart his cheeks. It was an amazing fantasy come true… and the only price was that he had to let his wife explore as well. Which wasn't a price, was it? He was happy for her.

Elena's tongue found his anus. So dirty. So slutty. Surely Meg wasn't doing anything this crude, this lewd. Or was she? Was she letting David tongue her ass? Was she rimming him? Again, his wife forced her way into his mind and he imagined her kneeling behind David, doing to her lover what Elena was doing to him.

Too much. He exploded suddenly in Zoe's mouth. He had an urge to apologize, but Zoe's excited moan seemed ample evidence that she was not only *not* angry, but actually relished it.

"Share, bitch," Elena ordered playfully.

She scooted beside Zoe and the two women melded into a passionate kiss, passing Mal's seed back and forth between them.

"Wanna taste?" Zoe offered to Mal. Her tongue was still coated with jism.

"No, but I'll taste something else."

He took each girl by one hand and led them over to the bed. They scooted up toward the headboard, side-by-side, and resumed their kissing. Mal crawled up between Zoe's legs and eagerly attacked her hot twat with his mouth. She was very wet, her pussy tangy on his tongue. After a few moments he switched, tasting Elena now. She was just as excited, but her pussy was different, saltwater taffy. He went back and forth, relishing their flavors, their hard bodies squirming at his touch.

Finally Elena interjected. "We don't need you for *that.*"

He grinned. "Yeah, and what do you need me for?"

Elena flipped over onto her hands and knees and wiggled her gorgeous little ass at him. He was hard again. Zoe reached into her purse and pulled out a condom. She tore the wrapper and unrolled it over his hard cock. Then, as if to make things unmistakably clear, she reached down and spread her friend's pussy open, giving Mal a perfect, pink target for his first hard thrust.

Elena gasped. Mal grabbed her hips and pounded into her hard. Zoe rolled over onto her back, legs spread wide and pulled Elena's face to her own juicy snatch. It was like being in the middle of a porno.

It felt even more that way when Zoe suddenly announced, "My turn."

This time they maneuvered Mal onto his back. The girls mounted him face-to-face, Zoe riding his cock, and Elena straddling his face, the women kissing passionately as he fucked and licked them. Elena came first and rolled off. Mal pressed Zoe onto her back and as he plowed into her, Elena bent between them, lapping wetly at Zoe's clit. Zoe bucked and shivered as her own orgasm swept through her.

Elena seized Mal's cock. She tore off the condom and sucked him enthusiastically into her mouth. Zoe sat up and grabbed her friend's head, forcing her to blow Mal even faster. The sight of Zoe jerking him off with Elena's mouth was too much. He felt his ball tingle and before he knew it, he was spurting deep into the brunette's mouth.

"You slut," Zoe hissed when she realized Elena had swallowed it all herself. "I shared with you."

Elena chuckled. "You should just be thankful I shared him with you at all."

Mal sat back on the bed. It was weird to hear them talking about him as if he were, what, an object? He felt oddly used. Men weren't supposed to feel that way. If he ever complained about it, he'd be called a fag and worse. After all, this was every man's fantasy, right? And yet, as fun as was the sex, he felt oddly indifferent.

He watched the girls dress.

"Thanks Mal, that was a nice way to start the evening," Elena said as she squeezed into her skirt.

"You guys are still going out?" he asked.

They laughed.

"Of course. The night is still young. But this was a fun way to bridge from happy hour to clubbing, didn't you think?" Elena replied.

He was just a way to pass a couple of hours.

Thirteen

Skyline Club made Pumped, the gimmicky club where they'd caught Tam at, seem quaint by comparison. At the time, she'd thought that the single room that Pumped took up was large. Skyline was palatial.

True to any Hollywood club, the line stretched down the block, and for a moment, Meg wondered if they'd get in before morning dawned. Everyone in line was young and beautiful, dressed to impress—and succeeding more often than not. The dresses that these women wore made Meg's LBD feel like a trench coat.

Not that it was. Not even close. She thought that after wearing her tight, little power suit all day, she would have gotten used to short skirts. She never did, and her party dress was even shorter. Stepping out of the cab, she was very careful not to open her legs, and almost stumbled out when she did.

"Careful now," David said, catching her.

"I'm not about to flash this crowd," Meg said with a laugh.

"But what a great story that would make. *Lawyer of Melanie Anderson, actress known for flashing her lady parts throughout town, gets caught flashing her lady parts.*"

Meg couldn't help but laugh. "*Lady parts?*"

He leaned in with a grin. "We're in public. Must keep up appearances."

Meg looked solemn and nodded. "Of course." Then she burst out laughing.

Truth was, she was more nervous than anything else. She'd had a glass of wine with dinner, but nothing more. She wanted to be more sober than last night—especially if tonight was going to stretch long into the morning, as she suspected.

Somehow, David had convinced her to go without panties tonight—again. She'd insisted on a bra, even though he tried to convince her to skip that, too. If she was going to dance at all, this dress and her large breasts demanded it. Not that her four-inch heels would let her dance too much. Already, her feet were killing her.

David regarded the long line for a moment, then took her arm and marched them up to the front. "Hi, we should be on the list," he said to the gorilla of a bouncer manning the door.

The guy didn't bother consulting his clipboard. He just looked them up and down and seemed about to tell them to get lost when David said, "We're Melanie Anderson's attorneys. Check, if you don't believe me."

The guy thumbed his nose. Again, he didn't consult the clipboard, but whatever David had said was enough. "Go on in. If she doesn't recognize you, I'm having you thrown out myself." He turned to Meg, his face splitting into a smile more charming than she thought him capable of. "You're free to stay."

Meg returned his smile. "Thank you. You hear that, David? You better hope Melanie remembers her *junior* attorney."

It was actually a nice reminder of the true balance of power. David and his dominant streak may have turned her on now, but back in the real world, she was his boss.

They walked into the Hollywood nightclub and into a wall of

sound. Again, Meg couldn't help but draw comparisons to Pumped. Skyline was the club that Pumped wished it could be, had it been born on the West Coast. Rather than one main dance floor, it was made up on three different floors, each large enough to contain the entirety of most other clubs. The main floor spun house music, strobes battering the undulating crowd like a choppy sea in a lightning storm. The second floor played hip-hop, wild and harsh and just as packed. The third floor was the most subdued, playing trance and drum and bass.

"We're never going to find her," Meg said as they searched the club. She'd seen a few famous faces in the crowd—or thought she had—but no Melanie.

"Probably not," David admitted. "Come on, let's go get a drink."

Meg was actually completely fine if they didn't meet up with the Hollywood starlet. She didn't like it, but the idea of Melanie and David flirting drove her crazy with jealousy. This place already made her feel old. When David turned his charm on their big-boobed, blond client, she'd feel ancient.

So a drink with just David sounded great—a way to prolong this fantasy just a few more hours. Tomorrow afternoon, they'd be flying home to the East Coast, where kids, marriage, and career all waited.

"Shots?" Meg asked, seeing what David has ordered for them.

"What better way to start a night at an LA club?"

Meg shrugged. Made enough sense. She picked up the shot glass. "To Melanie," she toasted.

David shook his head. "Fuck that. To a night with the hottest damn boss I could ever dream of."

The toast not only made her smile, but it made her wet. "That's something I'll drink to," she laughed.

The clear liquid in the shot glass tasted briefly of liquorice, then of fire. She coughed. "What the hell was that?"

"Something strong. Want to dance?"

She could already feel the heat of the shot filling her upper body with warmth. "Yeah, but first…." She pulled out her phone and held it out. "A pic to remember the night?"

David squeezed in beside her, his face close, his arm draped over her shoulder. She held the camera at arm's length, smiled up at it, and took the selfie.

"Kind of incriminating, don't you think?" David said to her. He was right, and his prudence was reassuring. He may have been a Millennial, but he also had a career ahead of him that he didn't want to jeapardize. That would make the transition home easier.

"Don't worry, I'm not going to post it on Instagram or anything. This is just for me."

"What if your husband sees?"

Meg bit her tongue inside her mouth. She almost let it out that Mal knew before she stopped herself. No, that wouldn't be a good idea, either, especially now that she knew how dominant David could be.

"Don't worry, I can be pretty discreet."

David collected her into his arms, pulled her close, and kissed her slow and deep. "That's one thing I like about you, Meg. Under those suits you wear, you hide a pretty fucking awesome secret."

Meg kissed him back, not caring who saw them. They were in LA. No one knew them.

Before they hit the dance floor, Meg shot a quick text off to Mal.

[Megan]: Just got here. No sign of our starlet. Having fun.

And with the text, she attached the selfie of her and David.

*

The text came in close to 1:30 in the morning. Mal had actually been dozing when it arrived. Turned out that wild sex with two women after barely getting any sleep the night before was enough to tire him out, no matter what his wife was up to.

When he saw the picture, though, any thought of sleep fled. The photo was proof that this was real—that Meg was out with another man. And judging from the way she was smiling into the frame, she was excited.

He spent a long time analyzing the photo. Her eyes were lined with darker make-up than he was used to, her lashes long, her lips glossy and pink. It had been an age since he'd seen her in her black dress, and it had never looked so good on her. Her tits literally spilled over the top, which hung low on her pale, freckled body.

David's arm rested casually over her shoulder, an act that could have signified nothing more than drunken friendliness. Mal knew better, though. He saw the act for what it was: a possessive one. David had laid claim to Meg, and that arm was his stake in the ground. Jealousy knotted in Mal's gut, that a man would presume as much with his wife.

And yet every time he looked at that arm, the way David rested a couple fingers on the bare skin of her chest, the way David was looking more at Meg than at the camera, Mal's cock grew hard.

They'd just gotten there. That put it at 10:30, which felt early for the LA night scene, but late in every other practical way. What had they done since 10:30? Had dinner, of course, but had they gotten ready together? Had they fucked prior to hitting up the nightclub, using each other like Elena and Zoe had used him earlier? Was sex part of the pre-party?

Mal climbed out of bed. Any hope of sleep was gone. He started to text her back, then stopped himself. Last night, he'd texted over and over again, only to receive nothing, and when they finally had a chance to talk, she'd put it off for when she got home. Meg was out there, having fun, and seemed to want to be left alone.

That thought grated on him one moment, and turned him on the next. He wanted to be included, but then thought about Meg letting loose and being wild with David, and Mal was all turned on again. It was very confusing.

No sign of our starlet, she'd texted. Melanie Anderson. It was still surreal that Meg was out there partying with the former Hollywood It Girl at all. Meg and Mal weren't the type to rub elbows with the rich and famous. They saw that world at the cinema—or in the tabloids, as was the case with Melanie most of the time—not out at clubs.

Before Mal realized what he was doing, he booted up his laptop and did a search for Melanie Anderson. She came up instantly, of course. It may have been several years removed from her last major movie—and even longer since her stint with Nickelodeon—but she was still very much in the spotlight.

Like most Hollywood starlets, she'd gone through a myriad of different looks over the years: she'd been a brunette, a redhead, a blonde. Currently, she was a blonde, which was probably closest to her real hair, long and wavy and bottled. She had doe-like blue eyes—expressive eyes, intelligent eyes that made it hard to write her off as another blond bimbo in Hollywood.

That was the most frustrating thing about Melanie. She was smart. She possessed acting talent that could have landed her on the A-List for years to come. Yet she was as reckless as any child star out there. LiLo, Britney, Miley—Melanie ranked right up there among the best. A scan of the pictures that came up on Mal's browser testified to as much.

He clicked one, showing Melanie getting out of a limo. She wore a silver dress that was probably illegal in public, short enough that it didn't even come close to covering her up. And of course she didn't wear panties, her bare snatch on display for the paparazzi. In the photo, she was sticking her tongue out at the camera.

Another photo showed Melanie hanging out on some rich guy's yacht. She was in a thong bikini, but had left the top off, and had both hands raised in the direction of the telephoto camera. One hand held an enormous glass bong. The other was flashing her middle finger.

But if you looked past her self-destructive behavior, there was a truly talented artist inside of her. The movie roles she'd chosen in her late teens and early twenties—while being YA garbage—suggested that there was more to this blonde that a pretty face and a tight body. She could have done something big with her life. Instead, it seemed like she was on a mission to fuck up everything she had. This para-sailing stunt that Meg was defending her on was just the latest incident.

Mal clicked through a few more photos of her before heading to bed. She had a body more like a pinup model than a Hollywood waif. She had curves, hips, an ass, and incredible tits. In many ways, she reminded him of a younger, blonder Meg.

That made Mal laugh. What would Meg think of herself being compared to Melanie Anderson? He couldn't think of anyone more different than those two.

*

David pulled Meg close, their legs interlocked, their eyes on one another. The crowd pressed in around them from all sides, each locked in their own worlds just inches away. Strangely, it all felt so intimate to Meg. *Alone in a crowd,* she thought as David's hand crawled over her ass.

They'd been dancing for a couple hours now, on and off, with still no sign of Melanie. They'd tried the main room for a while, then moved up to the hip hop floor. That had been fun, and it turned out David was pretty good with his hips. They were now on the top floor, the trance that they danced to reminding her of the raves she'd attended during her crazier youth.

The top floor had the tallest ceiling. Pinpoints of light played across the vaulted ceiling, simulating a starscape that LA didn't have due to smog and light pollution. But it wasn't the ceiling that was most impressive about this floor. No, what was most striking was the huge windows that made up the far corner of the club. They must have been forty feet high, reminding her more of an airport atrium than a dance club. And out beyond those windows was what gave the club its namesake: the LA skyline.

The corner was where the lounge was, sofas and chairs, small tables, pretty cocktail servers flitting through the place to serve the ultra rich. David and Meg had looked there first for signs of Melanie, but couldn't see anyone looking like her at a quick glance, so they'd moved on.

"Bored of me so quickly?" David whispered in her ear. She looked away from the windows, back at David.

"Sorry, I can't stop looking out there. It's beautiful."

"It's pretty cool," he acknowledged, looking right at her. "But not beautiful."

Meg hated herself for blushing at the compliment, but she blushed anyway. "You're right. What's beautiful is right here." She squeezed his cock through his pants, giggling at how naughty that felt. He wasn't hard, but he wasn't soft, either, and even after last night and in the bathroom at lunch, she couldn't wait to get him inside her again. He'd denied her after the case was done and after dinner, promising that he'd make it up to her later.

"And right here," David added. His hand slid up under her dress. She felt the dress pull along her thigh, reaching down to grab it before it got too high. "I could fuck you right here on the dance floor," he said.

Her body burned at the thought. No, that would be too much. Too far. What if they got caught? What if they got thrown out?

"Don't worry, Meg, I'm not that crazy. Just a little." With that, he pressed his fingers against her shaved pussy. She shuddered, looking around wildly.

"David…."

"You're wet," he said. "Naughty, naughty."

He traced his fingers along her lips, circling her clit without touching it. She shut her eyes, then opened them quickly when she realized where she was. "We can't…do this…." Talking at all became tough.

"We can't?" David asked. "Feels like I am."

"You know what I mean."

He pressed his middle finger inside of her. She gasped, moving as close as she could get against him. Around her, dancers danced, oblivious.

"Don't worry, I think most of the attention is on those two over there," David said, looking over her shoulder.

Meg followed his eyes, where a couple of young women were tangled in each others arms, their lips open in a deep, girl-on-girl kiss. He was right, most of the dance floor that wasn't into their partners was looking at the faux lesbian show.

"You know they're just trying to get attention, right?" she said, turning away from them.

"You know something about that, do you?" David pressed his palm against her mound as he fingered her deeper. "You never answered me earlier. Have you ever been with another woman?"

She hadn't, but there was this one night, back in college, when she and a friend got a little drunk and were trying to make an impression on a couple of guys. Much like the two behind her, they ended up making out in public. It had worked, and they ended up taking those guys back to their place, but that was as far as the lesbian show went. In the light of the morning, though, she regretted doing it. It felt a little desperate. Even back then, she had a very clear image of the woman she wanted to be—strong, successful, intelligent, independent. A cry for attention like that worked against the image she was building.

Thing was, David challenged it, too. David had already dismantled that persona. He'd made her blow him before the trial this morning. He'd fucked her into unconsciousness last night. With David, she didn't worry about who she *should* be.

So rather than answer him as Meg the Attorney, she found herself reverting back to the girl who'd kissed her friend to make an impression. "I've kissed a girl...."

"And did you like it?" Somehow, David managed to ask the question in a way that made her knees quiver, despite the Katy Perry song.

"I did it for a boy."

"I bet *he* liked it," he said.

"Oh, he did. Boys are easy like that."

"*So* easy," he agreed, his lips already descending over hers. As they kissed, he added a second finger to her pussy. For a long moment, the world went soft. She still heard the trancy beat, still saw the strobes light up behind her eyelids, still felt the press of strangers around her, but in that moment, all she cared about was the man she was pressed up against.

His lips moved away from hers, traveling down her neck. Meg swung her head from side to side, one with the beat and his soft touch. His fingers danced inside of her, seeming to find the rhythm of the room, too. She stopped caring who looked. Stopped caring about anything but how good her body felt and how naughty it was to be doing this in plain sight.

"You know what I can't wait to do?" he whispered in her ear.

His hand shifted under her dress, his fingers coming out and his thumb pushing inside of her. She groaned. Even though two fingers were thicker than the one thumb, there was more power in the single digit.

"Ever had it back here?" he asked.

Confused, she began to ask what he was talking about when his slippery fingers tickled across her asshole. Her entire body tightened, from the arches of her feet to the muscles in her neck.

"N-no," she whispered.

He pressed the tip of his index finger into her tight opening. Stars flashed behind her eyelids, although she couldn't be sure if it was the club's lights or something exploding inside of her.

"Good, because I want to be your first."

She tried to form something clever to say, to challenge him, to deny that she was his plaything. But she couldn't. All she could do was feel his finger penetrate her ass and wonder if she could take the full girth of his enormous cock back there. There was no way, but she knew then and there that she was going to try.

In the guise of dancing, he shimmied down her body, crouching to the floor. On his way up, though, he dipped in and ran his tongue along her slit.

Meg shuddered, feeling herself on the brink of an orgasm. Cold panic descended over her as she realized where she was. She shivered. David rose to his full height, sliding a hand behind her neck to pull her against him. At the same time, his free hand returned to her pussy, two fingers jamming inside of her.

"Come," David ordered. His command was like steel. "Now."

Meg gasped, her willpower crumbling. David kissed her before her moan betrayed her. The wall of sound around them swallowed the rest. For a perilous instant, she didn't care who heard. Who saw. Who knew. She could have been up on the DJ stage, legs spread, as David finger banged her, and she wouldn't have cared.

Her climax swelled, peaked, then ebbed just as quickly. The song transitioned. Suddenly, she was painfully aware of what had just happened. Heat touched her cheeks. Looking around, she saw one guy giving her a knowing look. Her face grew even hotter.

"I need to use the bathroom," she mumbled, not daring to look at the guy.

David grinned at her. The least he could have done was look bashful. "Go ahead. I'll meet you by the bar with another round."

"Yes. Another round sounds about right."

She pushed her way through the throng without meeting anyone's eyes. They were obstacles in her way more than people, and those obstacles were suddenly smothering her.

She was thankful that the bathroom was empty when she pushed in. She went to the mirror and splashed water on her face. Looking up, she met her eyes. *What the hell are you doing?* she asked herself silently. *You're a professional woman. You're acting like…like your reckless client, Melanie.*

As if she'd been summoned, the door swung open and Melanie Anderson entered. Like nearly every woman in the club, the blonde wore a miniscule party dress. Tonight's was a blood red halter dress that matched the bright shade of her lips and left very little to the imagination. The woman was a bombshell, and even Meg's imagination went dirty when looking at her in that little dress.

"Oh, hey. There you are," Meg said.

Melanie looked up at Meg as if seeing her for the first time. She regarded Meg blankly before realizing who she was. "Megan Trammell? Wow, you look...hot."

Meg blushed. "Call me Meg, please."

A smile spread across Melanie's face. "Okay," she said brightly.

Meg had had very little interaction with the starlet, but already she understood why Hollywood was still so enamored with the blonde. Seeing her smile made Meg want to smile.

"Thank you *so* much for all your hard work. You saved my life."

Before Meg could do the modest thing, Melanie enveloped her in a deep hug. Her hair smelled like fresh flowers, and there was no mistaking her full breasts pressed up against her own. Meg returned the hug awkwardly.

"And I'm so glad that you made it out here!" Melanie smiled after the hug. "Did you bring that cute guy with you?"

Meg pushed down the flick of jealousy. "He's here. Out by the bar, getting me another drink, actually."

"Awesome! You guys can join me in the VIP lounge." Melanie reached into her little red clutch and pulled out some lip-liner. Meg just stood there, watching the young woman touch up her lips, unsure of whether she was waiting or if she should leave.

"It's pretty cool here. The view is great."

Melanie shrugged. "It's okay. Too much glare though." She slipped her lip-liner back into her purse and pulled out what looked like a tube of lipstick. "Maybe after we get some drinks, I could show you the view from my house. Now there's a view."

Meg's heart began to race at the thought of going back to Melanie's place. It was probably innocent, but her mind immediately went to the stories she'd heard in the tabloids.

Melanie unscrewed the cap of the little silver tube she held and pulled out an even smaller spoon. On the spoon was a mound of white powder. Meg froze, her eyes wide. She was intensely conscious of how hard her heart was beating against her ribs. Then, as casually as she had touched up her lips, she lifted the spoon to her dainty nose and sniffed hard.

"Want a bump?" she asked, meeting Meg's eyes in the mirror.

Meg licked her lips. She'd done coke once before, but that was long ago, when she was a different person. She'd enjoyed the experience—probably too much—but it was too expensive a habit and she was too scared that she'd get addicted.

The moment hung thick between them. Meg suddenly felt like she was that twenty-year-old again, younger than Melanie, not ten years her senior.

"I'm good for now," she said, suddenly fearing the starlet's judgment.

If she judged, Melanie didn't show it. She just shrugged and recapped the tube. "Plenty of night left to party," she said. She snapped her purse shut, checked her nostrils for signs of residue, then smiled. "Come on, go grab your sexy assistant and meet me in the VIP room."

Fourteen

Meg found David at the bar and led him toward the VIP section. Another bouncer, another set of velvet ropes, a heavy black curtain to shield those inside from scrutiny by the ordinary patrons. But before they could explain who they were, Melanie herself burst through the drapes, followed a moment later by a slender, pale, young man.

"God damn it, Mel, what the hell is wrong with you?"

Melanie had a wild look in her eyes. She spotted Meg and made a beeline for her. The young man followed.

Melanie seized Meg by the forearm and turned triumphantly.

"This is my lawyer, Logan, and if you don't keep the fuck away from me, she's going to sue your fucking ass."

He looked Meg over, his expression some mixture of arrogance and insolence. Meg recognized him. Logan Donovan, another young star better known for late night misadventures than any screen successes.

"*That's* your lawyer?"

"Yeah, and she's one motherfucking, bad-ass bitch. You do not want to mess with her."

Meg was momentarily flattered, but then realized Melanie had no real idea what she was talking about. Still, testament to her acting skills, Logan seemed momentarily frozen. He shook it off quickly. He'd been getting away with too much for too long to be easily scared.

"Melanie, stop the shit, okay? Fuck, what's the matter with you?"

He reached out for the starlet. She squirmed out of his grip. She turned to Meg. "Tell him," she hissed.

Meg had no idea what was going on. Still, she interposed herself between Logan and Melanie.

"Mr. Donovan," she began in her best courtroom tone, "pursuant to Ms. Anderson's allegations concerning improprieties in your mutual enterprise, you are hereby apprised of her intention to seek judicial intervention should you continue in your harassment."

He stopped short. He eyed Meg.

"You don't know who you're messing with," he hissed. But obviously Meg's officious tone had put him off balance. "Fuck this shit," he groaned. He disappeared back into the VIP section.

"Yeah, fuck you!" Melanie screamed at him.

A small crowd was gathering.

Meg grabbed the younger woman by the shoulder. "Come on, we should get out of here."

Melanie looked over at Meg, and then at David. She grinned. "Yeah, let's."

*

Melanie led them through a back exit to a waiting limo. Meg breathed a sigh of relief. So many of these young stars liked to drive themselves, even though it led to endless problems with drunk driving arrests and accidents. Hopping in the back, Meg was suddenly aware of the strangeness of the situation—just her, David, and Melanie Anderson, of all people, driving west of the city, up in the hills of Topanga Canyon.

Melanie had put on some music, a Pandora station heavy on Beyonce and Kanye, and sloppily mixed them Vodka-Bombs. She held up her glass to Meg. "You were pretty good in there."

David laughed. "Yeah, Meg has a gift for bullshit."

Meg gave him the finger, though with a smile. "I still have no idea what that was about."

Melanie gave a dismissive wave. "Oh, Logan's an asshole. He thinks that just because we've fucked a few times and the tabs think we're a couple, it gives him a right to get up in my face…. Whatever."

Meg and David exchange a quick glance.

"Anyway," Melanie continued, "what about you two? You married?"

"Uh, no," Meg answered as she awkwardly slid her left hand into her lap to hide her wedding band.

"Not to each other," David added.

"But you *are* fucking," the young woman persisted.

Meg blushed. "That's none of your business." She glanced over at David, who was grinning. *Idiot.*

Melanie nodded at the answer. Then continued undeterred. "So how does that work? Does your husband know?"

"I think you have the wrong idea—"

"Oh please, lady, there is no way you're not fucking. Not with those titties hanging out, and plus, I think I saw a flash of gash when you got into the car."

"You'd know," Meg snapped.

Melanie smiled sweetly. "Exactly."

"So, what is it? You a swinger?"

"What do you care?" Meg countered.

Melanie replied, "I'm an actor. I study people."

You're a pretentious twit. "Seriously, What do you care?" Meg insisted, getting annoyed.

Melanie smirked. "Well, now that Logan cockblocked me, I'm trying to figure out what my options are for a little fun."

Meg blushed.

"What? You didn't think I wanted to talk about my case, did you?" She paused. "So?"

Meg gave her a puzzled look.

"Jesus, lawyer lady. So is slim here a sport fuck, a group marriage, what?"

Meg sighed. Melanie wasn't going to let go.

"Look, I'm married, but my husband and I have an understanding, I guess."

She glanced over at David who was suddenly wide-eyed.

"So you can just fuck whoever you want?" Melanie asked.

"No. It's not like that. It's…. Look, it's none of your business."

"Oh come on, we're among friends. Anyway, I'm your client. This is covered by attorney-client privilege."

Meg rolled her eyes. "That protects your secrets, not mine."

"Whatevs. Look, I'm just curious. So hubby knows you're here with boy toy…." Melanie looked over at David. Meg followed her gaze. "Ooh, he doesn't like that," Melanie said with a smirk.

"No," he replied.

"So *she's* your toy?"

"No," Meg replied.

"Yes," David insisted, louder.

"You have a big cock?" Melanie guessed.

David nodded. He was trying and failing to look nonchalant.

Melanie laughed. "Prove it."

He smirked and began tugging at his zipper.

"He loves showing it off," Melanie said to Meg.

Meg rolled her eyes. "Yeah, he's very proud of it."

"Think he can take us both?" Melanie asked.

Meg groaned. Things were getting out of control.

Melanie smiled and nodded. She was looking in David's lap. "Okay, that is about the biggest horse cock I've ever seen on a white guy."

He was stroking it slowly.

"Now your tits, ladies," David suggested.

Melanie laughed. "Chillax, Mr. Ed, and put that thing away. We're almost at my place."

The limo pulled up through the security gate and drove up a long, winding driveway, fringed with California pines. They crested a hill and saw the house. Surprisingly modest in size, it was modernist, white, boxy, all windows and straight lines. The landscaping, visible in the subdued accent lighting, conveyed the impression of wilderness, but was too tight for that, every shrub in the right place, trimmed to be just natural enough, but not too much.

As Melanie moved to the door, Meg leaned in toward David. "We should get out of here," she suggested.

David laughed. "Boss, *you* may get invited to threesomes with Hollywood stars on a regular basis, but I don't. Come on, it'll be a story you can tell your grandkids."

She shook her head. "Yeah, David, nothing grandkids like more than a story about grandma hooking up her boy toy and a coked up actress."

"I'm not a boy toy," he replied. "Coked up?"

Meg brought her pinky to her nose. "Yup."

David groaned. "Fuck, that's hot."

"Out of control turns you on?"

He nodded. "Of course! Come on Meg. Tonight, you're not a

lawyer, you're not a wife, you're not a mom; you're a hot, crazy slut."

"I'm not, you know." Though, Meg was oddly excited that he thought of her that way.

He laughed. "You *are!*"

"So, you two coming in?" Melanie chimed from outside.

*

Mal woke up with a start. How did swingers deal with it? It was 4:00am. His wife was across the country, with another man, doing… God knows what. It was impossible not to think about it. His time with Elena was a sexy distraction, but only that. Even when they were together he was periodically reminded of Meg, but the moment he was alone, thoughts of his wife consumed him. It should be the reverse, right? Elena his obsession, his wife the distraction. That's how affairs work. That's the fun of it, the crazed excitement of someone new, different, unexpected.

It wasn't working out that way. Mal groaned. Just a few hours ago, he'd had two women *at the same time*. It was every man's fantasy. And not just two women, but two *hot* women. And not just two hot women, but *two hot, uninhibited women*. They squabbled because when he'd come in Elena's mouth, she'd swallowed it rather than share his load with her friend. You couldn't write that. No one would believe it. And yet, instead of reliving the moment or thinking ahead to his next encounter with Elena…and Zoe…all he could think about was his wife, naked, in bed with another man, his cock plunging over and over into her sweet pussy.

Mal forced a chuckle. Meg probably felt the same. Neither one of them was built for this. A fun, crazy experiment, but surely once she got home, that would be it. He had no real regrets, but for Mal, it was more exciting to think about him and Meg in bed, giggling about their wild past than it was to think about another encounter with Elena.

He grinned. He couldn't wait for his wife to come home.

*

What the hell am I doing here? The thought swirled through Meg's mind. Holding hands with sexy, young David, following Melanie Anderson—Melanie Anderson!—on a tour of her Topanga Canyon house, with its huge deck, overlooking the rough beauty of the dry, scrubby, California hills. And then up the polished, bleached wood stairs to Melanie's huge bedroom. White carpeting, a huge bed on a raised platform, floor-to-ceiling windows.

Melanie had a bottle of champagne; David was holding three flutes as well as Meg's hand. She popped the bottle open and took a big swig, frothy wine bubbling from her mouth and dripping down her chin. David took the champagne from her.

"Fuck the bubs, horse cock, whip it out," she demanded.

David chuckled, but took his time and poured three glasses.

"Tits first," he insisted.

"My tits are worth more than your prick," Melanie replied.

He laughed. "Maybe at the movies. But not here. Anyway, Meg's got nicer."

Melanie laughed. "Oooh, we have a titty throw down. You up for it, Meg?"

"I've had three kids," Meg replied. But the situation was exciting. And fuck it, she knew she had nice boobs. "But okay."

Meg went first. She yanked her dress off her shoulders, taking the bra straps down at the same time. She shot David a glance, but focused on Melanie as she slowly exposed her large breasts.

Melanie nodded, impressed. "Those are real?"

Meg smiled. "Yeah."

Melanie laughed. "Damn, what are the odds? My two lawyers have world class tits and a world class cock. Okay, but how about these?"

Melanie reached down and yanked her blouse up over her head. She wasn't wearing a bra. She didn't need one. Her tits were big and perfect in a way that is only possible at twenty-something, full, rounded, high, with big, erect nipples.

Meg had to laugh. David was going back and forth between them with his eyes. For all his bravado, he too was out of his depth. He recovered fast though.

"Stand side-by-side," he…suggested? Ordered?

It was weird, but Meg never thought of refusing. Nor, apparently, did Melanie. They moved toward each other and turned to face David, shoulder-to-shoulder, breasts bare.

He approached them. His left hand cupped Melanie's right breast, his right hand on Meg's left tit. He lifted their heavy boobs, his thumb circling their nipples.

"So who wins?" the actress asked.

David seemed to take his assignment seriously, fondling the two sets of full breasts before him, tweaking their nipples, weighing, squeezing, caressing.

"I think I'll need to see them in action."

"You got a baby for us to breastfeed?" Meg snarked.

David gave her nipple a firm squeeze. "I was thinking more about how they bounce when you ladies take turns riding my cock."

Melanie turned toward Meg. "Is he always like this?"

"Pretty much," Meg replied with a shrug.

She couldn't help but reflect on how badly she'd misjudged him. The idea that he'd serve as a docile boy toy so obviously misguided now as to seem laughable. She might be a partner in a law firm, and Melanie a world famous actress, but Meg knew that he'd be calling the shots tonight and that she and the younger woman would deny him nothing. The power of the cock, Meg mused darkly.

"You might as well get the rest of your clothes off," he suggested.

Melanie chuckled as well, but it was obvious she was having similar thoughts as Meg. She shimmied out of her clothes, standing proudly naked, hand on hip. Melanie and Meg had very similar bodies, though Melanie was a little taller and had a mane of long, blond rather, than reddish, hair. Like Meg, she was completely shaved.

"You two could be sisters," he noted. "Show her, Meg."

Meg shrugged. *In for a penny, in for a pound.* She eased her own dress over her hips and let it fall to the ground.

"Very nice," David said.

He handed them each a glass of champagne. Melanie gestured toward the bed, and the two women sat on the edge.

"Now you," Melanie suggested.

David grinned. He drained his own glass of champagne and set down the flute. He approached the women, who regarded him eagerly.

He slowly unbuttoned and peeled off his shirt.

"Not bad," Melanie commented. "But give us the main course."

He grinned.

"Kiss first."

Meg shook her head. "No way."

He laughed. "Oh Meg, you know you two are going to be doing *a lot* more than kissing tonight, right?"

"You've never been with a girl?" Melanie asked, shocked.

"There are a lot things Meg's never done that she's going to do tonight," he replied.

Meg remembered what David had threatened...promised on the dance floor. He couldn't be serious. There was no way he'd be able to put his huge prick into her ass.

Melanie cut her off before she could reply, leaning in and kissing Meg wetly on the mouth. She tasted champagne on Melanie's soft lips, the other woman's insistent tongue probing gently for an opening. Meg was aware of David leaning in for a better view, his pants tenting with his excitement. Meg gasped in surprise as Melanie's hand slid between her legs. Melanie took the opportunity to press her tongue into Meg's mouth. David came closer, his fingertips trailing over Meg's hard nipples. She knew she should stop it, insist they go, but it was so tempting to just...let...go....

Melanie slipped a finger inside her. When had she gotten so wet? David's fingers squeezed her nipples harder. Meg moaned, and sucked forcefully on Melanie's thrusting tongue. Melanie growled excitedly and climbed into Meg's lap, wrapping her arms around Meg's head. The two women kissed passionately, grinding against each other, their big tits mashed together. It had happened so fast, but somehow felt so right.

David shucked off his pants, his huge prick jutting out from his body at a ninety degree angle. He stepped in close and ran his hand down Melanie's naked spine. She shuddered. His fingers slipped into her crack, pausing a few moments to tease her ass, before continuing their journey of exploration. Melanie moaned into Meg's mouth as David found her slit, wet and puffy with excitement. His fingers slick with Melanie's juices, he reached further, into Meg's lap, and slipped his finger into her sticky pussy.

Meg was reeling. She was making out with another woman, getting fingered by David at the same time. It was intoxicating. He moved beside them. Without even thinking, she reached out and closed her fist around his fat prick. He was rock hard and felt, if possible, ever bigger than before. She knew he wouldn't long be satisfied with using his hands on the two naked, ready women writhing before him.

"Which one of you wants it first?" he asked.

"Me!" Meg growled immediately, surprising herself with ferocity of her response.

"Great," he replied.

He pushed on Melanie's upper back, pressing the women onto the bed, Meg on her back, Melanie sprawled over her.

He swatted Melanie's ass. "Sit on her face."

Melanie scooted upward, thighs on either side of Meg's head. Meg had never been this close to another woman's sex. Melanie's gash was inches from her face, pink, wet, pulsing with excitement. But it was too much, too soon. Kissing a woman was one thing...eating her out was another.

"What are you waiting for?" Melanie demanded.

Meg couldn't form the words to answer. She just shook her head. She felt David lifting her legs, placing her ankles on his shoulders, his huge prick at her entrance.

Go slow, she thought, but the words didn't come out in time. He thrust in, hard, the sensation dizzying, overwhelming.

"Oh God," she gasped, shuddering.

There was no resisting it. He was too much, too good. He was taking her, possessing her body and soul. When he was inside her, she had no willpower of her own, no ability to refuse him. She came hard before she even knew what hit her. Then as her wits slowly returned, she heard him.

"Come on, baby, lick it," he urged.

His cock pressed into her again and again, deeper, harder. Meg looked up to see Melanie spreading her lips, exposing even more of her pink, juicy flesh. It was too much, too much. She wanted to scream and thrash about, pull his hair and claw at his back, but between David's grip on her legs, and Melanie straddling her face, she was trapped. She lashed out the only way she could, with her mouth, her tongue attacking and sucking on Melanie's wet, exposed twat.

Melanie gasped at the ferocity of Meg's assault. She hissed as Meg sucked hard on her swollen clit. She moaned as Meg licked deep into her drenched channel.

"Oh fuck, babe. Fuck yeah. Eat my pussy."

There were moments of lucidity between thrusts, when he pulled out and prepared another stroke, when Meg felt that emptiness and longing for him but also possessed the ability to process her surroundings, until he entered her again, and then all that existed was a feeling of being complete, possessed. A strobe-light effect, but with all of her senses, not just her vision. In those fleeting instants, she could taste Melanie, her salty tanginess, different, but not unpleasant. She could see the younger woman's enjoyment, the way her body twisted as Meg tasted her, the way her eyes closed when she sucked her clit. Giving oral to a man always felt submissive. In a good way, sexy. But she liked the sense of power that sucking on Melanie's pussy gave her. Melanie was moaning, louder, louder, grinding her pussy against Meg's face.

"Oh God, I need a cock," the younger woman gasped suddenly.

David was all too happy to oblige. Meg felt a surge of loss and jealousy as he withdrew his gorgeous prick from her hungry pussy. Still trapped beneath Melanie's crotch, she couldn't move as David released her legs. He climbed onto the bed, straddling Meg's chest. Melanie fell forward onto her hands and knees, her big tits dangling just past the top of Meg's head. And then, right in front of her eyes, inches away, she watched as David's amazing, glistening cock found its mark and plunged hard into the blonde's well-prepared pussy.

It was such a mesmerizing sight that it took Meg a few moments to realize David wasn't wearing a rubber. He'd fucked her, and was now screwing Melanie bareback. She knew she should be appalled, but all she could think about was how hot her view was. Melanie, a notorious party girl had surely experienced a wide variety of cocks, but based on her whimpering and moaning even she seemed taken aback by David's size. Her pussy seemed to be stretched to its limits as well, her labia clinging to his fat shaft on each stroke.

Meg craned her neck upward and sucked Melanie's clit into her mouth, her lips brushing against David churning cock. It seemed to give David an idea. He pulled out of Melanie, eliciting a desperate moan, and slowly pressed his cock into Meg's mouth. She couldn't take him deep in that position, but she did the best she could, sucking on the head of his cock, tasting a heady cocktail of her pussy, Melanie's, and David's pre-cum. After a few minutes, he withdrew from Meg's mouth and plunged back into Melanie's grasping cunt.

David went back and forth, back and forth. Melanie came first, gasping and grunting as he pounded her and Meg licked her clit, and then a moment later it was David's turn. Meg watched his balls tighten and his shaft pulse. He came with just the tip of his prick inside Melanie, so that his come immediately dripped out all over Meg's lips and face.

They gingerly unraveled and sprawled out on the big bed, naked, sweaty, gasping. David rose and refilled the champagne glasses, handing one to each of the women. As they sipped, Meg couldn't help but notice that David was still visibly aroused.

"Don't get too comfy. I'm just getting started with you whores."

*

Meg knew she was an attractive woman. Enough men had told her, and even with her own share of nearly universal body issues, she could see it herself as well. But one thing she'd always envied Mal was his ability to stand around naked totally unselfconsciously. It was her luck to be spending time with two more natural exhibitionists.

Despite a wall of floor to ceiling windows giving out onto a canyon filled with other multi-million dollar mansions, Melanie and David seemed to have absolutely no compunction about prancing around in the nude. Melanie did have a gorgeous body, everything Meg had, except just a bit tighter, firmer, as befitting a childless woman over a decade younger.

And David…. She realized now those pants were no accident. What did he say to his tailor? *Cut it a little loose around the arms for comfort, and make sure the pants show off my package?* She stopped short in her musings about his vanity. It had worked after all, because here she was, freshly fucked, and as she was watching him, thinking about more.

Melanie had gotten another bottle of champagne from downstairs and was also waving around her little cylinder.

"Who wants a pick me up?" she chimed.

David looked over at Meg.

Oh God, please don't try to talk me into it. She wasn't sure she'd be able to resist his blandishments about trying coke anymore than she was able to resist his sexual demands. She really *was* his slut…. But just for out here, just for California…. *Once we get back home….*

Again, her mantra. Once they got back home, things would go back to normal. Was she saying it because it was a comforting thought? Or because she was trying to convince herself?

"Naw, we don't need Meggy hopped up for what's next. We need her mellow. Got any weed?"

Melanie laughed. "Of course. This is Cali, baby."

She reached into her bedside table and pulled out a slender vaper.

"Uh, what's next?" Meg asked.

David smirked.

Meg felt a lump in the pit of her stomach. She thought back to the dance floor. She could almost feel again his finger inside her butt. She shivered.

"You know," he answered.

She nodded.

"Say it," he ordered.

"My ass."

Melanie had frozen, her face a mask of excitement. She seemed to be almost shivering in anticipation.

"You ever get butt fucked?" the actress asked.

Meg shook her head slightly.

Melanie sat down beside Meg. She filled the vaper and took a hit. She handed it to Meg and showed her how to use it. Meg took a hit. So much smoother than those joints and bongs she'd used back in college. No burn, no heat, just a cool mist and a delicious, smooth, mellow high.

"It's my fantasy," Melanie confided.

"Anal?"

Melanie laughed. "Ah, no. I mean, I've been doing it for years. Long story. You don't want to hear it. Well, maybe that's where it comes from. Anyway, the hottest thing for me is watching girls get ass fucked for the first time. It's my favorite porn."

Meg chuckled nervously. "That's a thing?"

"Everything's a thing?"

"I don't know if I can take him," Meg confided.

Melanie leaned in and kissed Meg softly on the lips. "You can't. That's what makes it so hot. It's gonna wreck you."

"You bitches talking about me?"

David was standing beside the bed, big prick dangling menacingly, an arrogant, yet attractively confident smirk on his face.

Melanie batted her eyelashes. "Of course, stud. What else is there to talk about?"

He grinned, in on the joke, yet getting a kick out of her response.

"Less talking, more sucking," he replied. And when the girls didn't immediately respond, he added, "It's not going to blow itself."

Melanie dropped off the bed and took his big prick in her hand. She licked the tip and then turned back toward Meg. "Come on, baby, let's get this thing nice and hard for your ass."

Meg shuddered and yet, as if under an irresistible compulsion, dropped to her knees beside the younger woman. They worked as a team on David's prick. His size made it easy. Even with Melanie bobbing up and down on the head of his cock, there was plenty of shaft left for Meg to lick and suck. They switched, now bringing his balls into the mix, kissing wetly in between.

"Do you have any lube?" he asked.

Melanie dove back across the bed and retrieved a tube of Aquaglide. She tossed it to David. He caught it and grinned at Meg.

"Slide back onto the bed," he ordered.

Melanie reached down and encouraged Meg back onto the mattress. They kissed again, tenderly.

"Just relax, baby," Melanie sighed.

Meg swallowed hard and nodded.

David pressed her legs back against her chest. He trailed his fingers gently up and down her still-swollen slit. He leaned forward and kissed her clit. Meg moaned softly. Then he teased lower. Meg tensed as his finger found her tight, little rosebud. He coated his finger tips with lube. Meg startled again as his now slippery finger circled, circled, and then firmly pressed inside her.

Melanie kissed her cheek. "Relax. Deep breaths."

Meg closed her eyes and thought back to the yoga techniques Mal had taught her to prepare for childbirth. Deep breaths, a focus on sensations, on controlling her muscles, her reactions, not as a matter of deliberation, but of attitude, of acceptance, come what may.

David sensed her surrender. He pressed a finger deep inside her. Her ass clenched in protest. Less in pain than in unfamiliarity. Melanie kissed her cheek, gently fondled her breast. He pumped his finger in and out, slowly, adding more lube until his digit slid in and out smoothly.

Okay, okay, I can do this. Meg's optimism faded when he added a second finger. Melanie again soothed her, caressing her cheek, kissing her forehead. Her other hand now playing with her nipples. In and out, again and again, lots of lube, his fingers stretching her out.

And then suddenly his fat prick was at the entrance to her ass. She looked down with trepidation, then over at Melanie panting excitedly. He thrust inside her. Just the tip and yet Meg gasped. She saw Melanie's face light up.

"Fuck her," the young actress growled. "Make her squeal."

David plunged in deeper. Meg writhed. Discomfort, definitely. Was it pain? Or just unfamiliarity? Meg wasn't sure. She felt an urge to scream, but was able to hold it in. Deeper. *Oh God.* The sensation of being stretched. That he might split her in two.

Another thrust. A moment of relief on the outstroke, and then that moment of madness as he plunged in still deeper. And again.

Meg cried out. "Oh God!"

Her whine seemed to excite David even more. He thrust in harder. She squealed, and Melanie gasped in excitement.

"It hurts?" Melanie asked, hopeful.

"Yes," Meg gasped.

"But you love it," David added.

"Yes!" Meg groaned.

He forced his cock in still deeper.

Meg cried out, but it didn't occur to her to ask him to stop. It was too good. Even with the pain, the loss of control, it was still amazing. A feeling of being so stretched, so full, so dirty, so slutty, so crazy.

"Fuck me," she hissed. "Fuck my ass." Melanie groaned excitedly. David thrust in deep.

"Ai!" Then after a moment. "Fuck me!"

Deeper, harder, Meg's ass screamed in protest. She squealed and cried out. Melanie's excitement grew, her hands and lips all over Meg's sweaty, shuddering body. David was fucking her now. Not slow, individual strokes, but hard, continuous fucking, his huge prick sliding easily into Meg's tight, virgin asshole.

Melanie licked her way down Meg's writhing form until she was just inches away from where David's huge cock plunged over and over into Meg's butt. Melanie leaned in and sucked hard on Meg's clit. Meg bucked. *Too much. Too much. Too much…. Oh my fucking God!*

David could feel her pussy clenching in orgasm from her ass. It was too much for him as well. He came hard, filling Meg's ass with his seed. She hissed as if scalded, the two of them writhing together.

As he pulled out, Meg felt drained, as if someone had sucked all of the life force out of her. She lolled on the bed, barely conscious. Her last memory was of Melanie desperately grasping David's cock, fresh out of Meg's ass, and sucking it deep into her mouth.

*

Later, after Melanie's driver had returned them to their hotel, Meg flitted in and out of sleep, stuck somewhere between consciousness and slumber. It was hard to distinguish the two. Her memories of the past few days were more outrageous, lurid, and surreal than her actual dreams.

She thought of Mal, generous, kind, funny, of her impatience to return to him, to laugh and cuddle as they shared tales of their adventures. But she also thought of David. Of her desires, achieved yet not fully sated. That sensation of having had enough, yet still wanting more. Confusing, disconcerting, unsteadiness on a storm-tossed ship, reaching for a prize and having it snatched away at the last moment, footsteps but no forward progress, shapes twisted, unmoored. Glimpses of the men in her life, and spinning, spinning, spinning....

*

Mal tossed and turned. He never slept well without Meg beside him. Something about the heat off her body, the way her weight shifted in the bed, her slow rhythmic breaths lulling him to sleep. And without that there, a feeling of cold emptiness.

But this wasn't like those other business trips or visits to family. Her absence this time felt heavier, less a temporary absence than a trial. That was the other meaning of experiment: a test-run, a try-out for something new, different. A silly thought, paranoid, unjustified. They were in this together....

He felt a twinge. The sentiment's fundamental inaccessibility forcing its way to the surface. They'd gone into it together. That was true. But the future is another thing, shaped by, but not bound by, the past or its understandings.

Meg had had a fling. So had Mal. But that was the past. The question remained. What was going to be the future?

About the Authors

Kenny Wright

I'm just a guy who writes what I like to read: steamy, explicit erotica that's just crazy enough to be true. I write romantic erotica. I write about characters that I like, and endings that feel natural. I write stories where husbands watch their wives get naughty. I write about MILFs and erotic games and loss of innocence. I believe in a world where men read and appreciate erotica, and hope to contribute to it word by word.

Find me online at www.kennywriter.com, or follow me on Twitter at @kennywriter. I also operate eroticaformen.com, which may or may not look like crap right now.

Ben Boswell

I am your typical family man with a wife and kids and an overactive imagination. I am a longtime reader and author of erotic fiction. I write in genres that I find exciting and arousing. Most of my stories are in the naughty wife, wife-watching genre, though occasionally I venture into other subject matter.

Reader feedback is what keeps me going. Please feel free to contact me at ben.boswell.author@gmail.com or visit my blog at benboswell.com. You can follow me on Twitter @BenBoswellAut.